DECK WITH FLOWERS

LARGE TYPE
FIC
CADELL

Elizabeth Cadell

Chivers Press • Thorndike Press
Bath, England   Thorndike, Maine USA

This Large Print edition is published by Chivers Press, England, and by Thorndike Press, USA.

Published in 1997 in the U.K. by arrangement with the author's estate.

Published in 1997 in the U.S. by arrangement with Brandt & Brandt Literary Agents, Inc.

U.K. Hardcover ISBN 0–7451–8844–3 (Chivers Large Print)
U.K. Softcover   ISBN 0–7451–8845–1 (Camden Large Print)
U.S. Softcover   ISBN 0–7862–0934–8 (General Series Edition)

The text of this Large Print edition is unabridged.
Other aspects of the book may vary from the original edition.

Set in 16pt. New Times Roman.

Printed in Great Britain on acid-free paper.

British Library Cataloguing in Publication Data available

Library of Congress Cataloging-in-Publication Data

Cadell, Elizabeth.
    Deck with flowers / Elizabeth Cadell.
        p.   cm.
    ISBN 0–7862–0934–8 (lg. print : sc)
    1. Large type books.   I. Title.
[PR6005.A225D43   1997]
823′.914—dc20   96–44926

CHAPTER ONE

Rodney Laird drove under the eighteenth-century arch that gave entrance to Belthane Mews, stopped his car in the cobbled courtyard, sat for some moments staring at the line of doll-sized houses, and then decided that he had misread his directions; Oliver Tallent could certainly not be living here.

His eyes went in wonder down the row. Number 1 was painted lilac, with a front door the colour of violets. Number 2, orange-coloured, had a lion's mouth as letter box, and window boxes filled with red plastic geraniums. The third in line had a red-and-white striped front door against which a gigantic figure 3 twisted like a silver serpent. The fastidious, un-frivolous Oliver living here? Not possible.

Then Rodney's eyes went to the fourth and last house in the row, and he knew he had come to the right place. Number 4 was an all-over, unadorned grey. Its aspect, in contemptuous contrast to that of its neighbours, was plain, cold, severe and withdrawn.

He drove the remaining few yards to the door, got out of his car and turned up the collar of his coat to keep out the falling sleet. He did not have to use the knocker; the door opened and Oliver, tall, grave and good-looking,

1

wearing a loose Japanese robe, invited him to enter.

'I'm late; sorry.' Rodney stepped into the warm hall. 'At least, the plane was late, and then I stopped to ring Angela and have a few words with her.' His eyes took in the robe. 'Judo session?'

'Comfort. Hang up your coat and come in and sit down.'

'Can't I have a look round first?'

'You can see it all from where you're standing.'

'So I can. Won't you feel a bit cramped after living for so long in that Kensington mansion?'

'I might, but I don't think so. The living room's what they call spacious, and there's a decent bedroom and bathroom. It's big enough for two.'

'Two? Oh, Cynthia. Her firm did the decorating, didn't it?'

'Yes. Inside and out.'

'You've made the neighbours look a bit gaudy. Don't they mind?'

'I've no idea. I don't know them.' Oliver led the way into the living room. 'Sit down. What'll you drink?'

'Gin and tonic and a slice of that lemon, and no ice. After a month in the States, I never want anything on the rocks again. When did you move in?'

'A couple of weeks ago. I'm sorry you don't like the decor.'

2

'Did I say so?'

'Not out loud. What don't you like about it?'

'Well, you know me. I'd like a few ornaments to fiddle with—and some pictures on the walls. You had some good pictures—what have you done with them?'

'In store. What you're trying to say is that you find it a bit stark.'

'Let's say I'm a chintzy chap. If Cynthia likes it, fine; she's the one who'll be living here.'

'Not Cynthia.'

'No?'

'No.'

'What went wrong?' Rodney asked, and bit off 'this time'.

'Well, I gave her a free hand with the decorating, and I paid her astronomical bill without protest, but I objected to her bringing her clients here at all hours to show them round.'

'And she objected to your objecting?'

'Yes. But I like the way she did the place. I asked for sober comfort, and I got it.'

'You did indeed. Very sober. What I feel it needs is to have Angela let loose in it for a day. She'd soon—'

He pulled himself up; he always tried to keep his sister's name out of his conversations with Oliver. Not, he mused, that it made any difference; her name never made the slightest ripple—as now: Oliver was absorbed in putting black olives into a dish.

3

Studying him, Rodney saw that he was beginning to have a settled, fortyish look, which was not surprising; he had always looked eight or ten years older than his age.

'We're both getting on,' he observed.

Oliver looked up.

'We are,' he agreed, 'but I'm getting on faster than you. There was always a touch of old-boy in me, and small-boy in you. Henrietta wouldn't believe you were as much as thirty.'

'Henrietta?'

'Henrietta Gould. She'll be here soon. You met her once at—'

'That's right. I met her,' Rodney said, and marvelled inwardly. Here was yet another in the series of women with each of whom Oliver had planned to settle down and raise a family. Except for their names, he mused, you couldn't tell them apart—all of them large, handsome and hard, and not one of them with any intention of being demoted to domesticity. Pauline, Ianthe, Georgina, then one with a loud voice whose name he couldn't recall, and then Cynthia, and now Henrietta. Why did a man as decent as Oliver attract the harpies?

'I've ordered dinner here, for three,' Rodney heard him saying. 'There's a good restaurant round the corner in Belthane Street—they send in meals. I ordered lobster salad—a bad choice on a night like this, but it's what Henrietta always asks for.'

'Perhaps I'm thinking of the wrong

4

Henrietta,' Rodney said hopefully. 'The one I met was living with that architect who—'

'That's over. She and I get on very well, but it's too soon to decide whether we want to put it on a permanent footing. Do you want anything to eat, besides olives?'

'Yes, please. Cheese biscuits, if you've got any. I'm pretty hungry. But I can't stay for the lobster salad, thanks all the same; I promised Angela I'd be back for dinner. She's cooked it specially. She—'

Once more, he broke off, once again he noted Oliver's total lack of interest.

The cheese biscuits were produced, and Oliver sat down.

'And now you can tell me about your trip,' he said. 'How did it go?'

'Very well, I think. But you never know with Americans—didn't you find that when you were over there? They're all so damned pleasant, and friendly, and hospitable that you find yourself forgetting there's business to be done. It seemed crude to mention that I was really there to push the Landini memoirs and try to assess how much splash they'd make when they're published.'

'I suppose you got some idea?'

'Yes. Big splash. There's been a lot about Madame Landini in the newspapers. The odd thing is that it isn't only the older generation that seems to know her name. I was told that her records still sell to young collectors. Has

5

she been letting you have the manuscript in instalments, as she said she would?'

'Yes. The later instalments are all neatly typed. I got her a secretary just after you left. There was a slight hitch at first.'

'I thought there might be. I suppose Claudius made a fuss when he realised that Madame Landini expected him to pay her secretary's salary?'

'That wasn't the hitch. He objected, of course, but he had to give in. The trouble was that the girl—her name's Nicola Baird— refused to live in, as Madame Landini wanted her to do. She said she didn't mind arriving early and working late, but she wouldn't take the job unless she could go on living in the room or rooms she rents somewhere in Pimlico.'

'And Madame gave in, like Claudius?'

'Yes. She seems to like the girl.'

'You've got the manuscript here, as far as it's gone?'

'Yes. I knew you'd want to take it home and read it.' Oliver opened a drawer and took out a file. 'It's a good deal easier to read now than it was in Madame's writing.'

'I'm afraid to ask—is it going on as well as it began?'

'Even better.'

'Thank God. How far has she got?'

'I suppose you could call it a kind of halfway point; she's just finished the account of her

6

husband's—her first husband's—death about twenty-five years ago. I didn't realise it had caused such a stir.'

'I could have told you. Last time I was at home, I told them that Claudius was publishing the Landini memoirs, and my mother and father talked about her for hours. I learned one curious thing: that my father actually took part in the search for the body. He was a sub-lieutenant at the time, and his ship was ordered to cruise up and down the Channel and he missed a weekend leave and so never forgot the event. He even remembered the name: Anton Veitch. I'm glad the book's holding up. I was afraid there might be a flattening after that magnificent start.'

'You needn't worry; the separate parts of her life all have the same interest. I'm not sure how far you read.'

'Her childhood as a Russian princess, and the Revolution. She and her parents were just about to flee.'

'Well, it goes on with their life in Paris, and her parents' death, and her discovery that she'd got this phenomenal voice. What impressed me, what'll impress you, is the easy transition from one stage to the next—the search for a teacher, the years of study, her early career—and then her marriage to Veitch, and his death. Why did she drop her title when she married Landini?'

'She said it was Landini's wish. She called

herself Princess Anna throughout her career. When she married Landini, she agreed to drop the title and be known as Madame Landini.'

'I see. There's still a lot to come—as I told you, the manuscript only takes the story up to her first husband's death.'

'Has Claudius seen any of it yet?'

'Yes. All there is. I would have preferred to keep it until you got back, but he asked for it, and as you hadn't given me any instructions, I had to let him have it. He gave it back to me yesterday and I tried to discuss some of the things I'd arranged for the book, but he wasn't listening—he'd gone back to the past, when he used to go to her concerts and sit spellbound. He kept muttering "What a voice, what a figure, what a woman", so I left him. Your glass is empty. Time for one more?'

'Yes. Thanks.' He opened the file. 'What's in the big envelope?'

'Illustrations. Photographs. Some letters she'd like reproduced, that kind of thing. Claudius hasn't seen those yet.'

'I'll go through them first.'

Oliver refilled his glass and Rodney's and was carrying them back to the sofa when the throb of a taxi sounded outside, and the knocker gave several loud thumps. Oliver went into the hall, and through the open door of the living room Rodney saw a tall girl he recognised as Henrietta Gould. She took off a fur coat, revealing a dark green trouser suit.

Oliver, having paid the taxi, carried her suitcase to the bedroom, leaving on the hall table the long cardboard box she had brought.

'Those are the flowers you sent me,' she told him. 'I couldn't bear to leave them behind at the office, so I put them back in the box and brought them here. Not,' she added, stepping into the living room and looking round it with her face puckered in distaste, 'that you could put flowers in this setting. I warned you, Oliver'—she turned to address him as he entered—'I *warned* you not to let that firm undertake the decorating. This looks to me like an outsize coffin.'

'In which case, flowers would be in order,' Rodney commented.

Her cold grey eyes came to rest on him, and the dislike he had felt on their previous encounter revived and grew stronger.

'You're Rodney Laird, of course,' she told him. 'We've met before. Oliver tells me you're publishing Madame Landini's memoirs.'

'D.S. Claud is, yes.'

'Nobody can make out why on earth she chose to let them do it. Any of the leading publishers would have jumped at the chance. Well, I hope the book will make you all rich. If the publisher makes a lot of money, then the literary agent ought to, and it's time Oliver had someone of Madame Landini's fame to act for. Could I have a drink? Rum and orange, please. I'm cold right through. I hope you ordered something warming for dinner, Oliver?'

'Lobster salad, I'm afraid.'

'For you, perhaps. Not for me,' she told him firmly. 'You must be out of your mind even to *think* of salad in weather like this.'

Rodney finished his drink, and rose.

'Sorry; got to be off,' he said.

She looked relieved. Putting down her glass, she told him she had met his sister.

'That is, I think so,' she said. 'Isn't her name Angela?'

'Yes.'

'I saw her at a party, I forget where. She's very pretty, isn't she?'

Spoken, Rodney thought with rage boiling up in him, like a woman well aware that in that direction she had nothing to fear. He picked up the file and walked into the hall to get his coat.

'Will you be at your office tomorrow,' Oliver asked, 'or will you wait until after the weekend?'

'Depends how long it takes me to read this. I've also got some unpacking and clearing-up to do. Thanks for the drinks. Be seeing you.'

He drove away. The sleet had turned to snow, but he lowered a window and drew in deep draughts of air to clear Henrietta out of his lungs. What was happening to Oliver, he wondered? In their schooldays he had been shy and awkward, but amusing. Oxford had loosened him up and until the last year or two, he had retained his good sense and judgment and something of his humour. Now he seemed to have given himself into the hands of a succession of women who were turning him into a professional escort. Perhaps he had felt the need for some distraction—he had worried about his job more than he cared to admit. He had a large income of his own, but the literary agency he had launched three years ago had only lately begun to find its feet. It was to have been Tallent and Laird, but it was still only Tallent, and Rodney could not for the life of him have said whether he would eventually join it—or not. He was aware that his future as Oliver's partner promised infinitely more than anything he could achieve by staying with the publishing firm of D.S. Claud, but he liked Claudius and found it impossible to make up his mind to leave him.

He closed the window and drove to the garage he rented close to the house in which he lived. Putting away the car, he walked a short distance up a narrow street to the shabby front door of Number 11—and as he went he could see, despite the darkness and the falling snow, the great changes that had taken place in the neighbouring houses since first he saw them.

He had come to London three years ago, and had at first searched unsuccessfully for a place in which to live. His inclination was towards Greenwich, whose history he had perhaps absorbed from his naval father. But residential Greenwich was expensive, and he widened his search until at last, wandering round Deptford, he came upon River Street. Something about the small, seedy, dilapidated rows of houses along it made him pause. Late Stuart, he guessed; they were of brick, and some had beautifully carved wooden brackets supporting hoods over the doorways.

He walked slowly along the street. He knew that many of the houses in this district had unexpectedly large interiors, having in Samuel Pepys' day been occupied by officials connected with the naval dockyard. As he went past Number 11, he glanced up and saw a card in one of the windows:

UPSTAIRS TO LET

He knocked. The knocker came off in his hand, and a short, stout, red-faced, aggressive-looking woman came to the door and asked him what he thought he was a-doing of.

'There's a notice upstairs saying—'

'Oh, that? You're the first wot's come since I stuck it up there six weeks since. Want to see the rooms?'

'Please.'

'Then gimme that knocker, an' come in. What's yer name?'

'Rodney Laird.'

'Mine's Mrs Major. No kids, and been a widder since the war, if you can remember back that far.'

He followed her up the two stone steps and found himself in a large hall. The stairs were of oak—neglected, but still stout English oak; these houses must have been built, he thought, when they were building ships for Charles the Second not far away. Upstairs, there were three small rooms and one large one; there was also a dingy bathroom, and a kitchen which Mrs Major told him had been put in for her mother, who had lived the last ten of her ninety-two years up here.

Rodney moved in. The largest room became his living room; one of the three smaller rooms was his bedroom. A space behind the bathroom he made into a lumber room in which he stored the more hideous pieces of Mrs Major's furniture, replacing them from sales or second-hand shops. When his arrangements and improvements were completed, he acknowledged that the rooms looked not at all like the expensive bachelor apartments seen in advertisements, but they fulfilled his two prime needs: space, and a view of the river. The river view was obtained through the small square of bathroom window, but however narrow the visible stretch of water, however muddy and crane-bordered, it was still the Thames.

He was barely installed when a house at the Greenwich end of the street was bought by an enterprising young naval officer and in no time at all transformed into a spruce bijou residence. Soon the house next to it and the one

13

opposite had been bought by his friends and their friends: River Street had been discovered. Prices soared and continued to soar. When two more houses in the street had been bought and converted, Rodney waited daily to be told by Mrs Major that she had decided to sell.

But Mrs Major, he found, had no intention of selling. For forty years she had reigned as undisputed queen of River Street. For forty years she had supervised her neighbours' births and deaths, arranged their marriages, directed their affairs, propped up the meek and abused the erring. In the Stuart Arms, at the end of the street, she had held court. Now she was dethroned. Her old friends and neighbours had sold their houses and were moving away, and the newcomers' interest in her was confined to the hope of getting her to do daily cleaning work for them. The Stuart Arms, in which she had spent so many convivial evenings, had become the meeting-place of bright young naval couples. Her bitterness and loneliness had hardened into a resolve to get her revenge in the only way that lay open to her: by refusing to sell her house, and staying to become the scourge of her new neighbours. Money, Rodney realised, could not bring her half the pleasure she got from bundling persistent house agents unceremoniously over the doorstep, or placing her overflowing dustbin outside Number 9, or hanging her undergarments to dry out of her front

14

windows, or pretending to wash the front steps and sending streams of soapy water along the pavement. Money could not buy her the triumph she experienced when hammering on the doors of houses at which smart cocktail parties were being held, and in lurid language ordering the owners of cars parked outside her house to remove them. Her dust-streaked windows and unwashed curtains were a blot on the surrounding smartness, and she was the terror of the street, and she was happy.

After living alone for a year and a half, Rodney had answered an unwritten appeal from his sister, and invited her to come up to London to keep house for him. Before her arrival, he and Mrs Major between them had kept the rooms in reasonable order. Now he opened the door of the living room, dropped his suitcase on the floor and stood looking at a scene which, familiar as it had become, still filled him with rage. Hair-drying equipment was spread over the carpet. An open work-basket on the floor spilled a colourful assortment of material. On a chair was a tray with the remains of tea. Along the mantelpiece stood bottles of cream, powder, nail varnish and hair spray. A vase of flowers, beautifully-arranged but long dead, stood on a corner table. In the centre of the crumb-covered carpet sat Angela, her hair falling over her eyes, her mouth full of pins, working on an outspread length of material.

This was home, he reflected, and he had seen it look worse. Somewhere between the starkness of Oliver's surroundings and the disorder of these rooms there was, he presumed, a middle course—a happy, happy medium. Some men came home, not to this mess, but to routine and order and a good meal.

His eyes went to his sister, still unaware of his presence, and for a few moments he studied her with detachment. Pretty; more than pretty. Lovely long lines, a deceptively delicate look, straight-falling fair hair. Attractive by most standards, he thought—but not by Oliver's. Since her schooldays, Oliver had been her ideal, but he had never looked at her. His lack of interest had not mattered down in Cornwall, but his total neglect of her after she came to London had hurt her. She was not a girl to pine, but she showed very little interest in other men.

She looked up and saw Rodney, and he thought she was going to swallow the pins. He was about to speak when a strong smell of burning took him swiftly across the room to the kitchen. She came in on his heels.

'Rodney, how wonderful to ... Oh Rodney, your *dinner*!'

He was lifting a smoking saucepan off the stove.

'What was it, when it was dinner?' he asked mildly.

'It was the most tender, the most expensive veal, done the way you said you liked it.'

'Not this way.' He put the saucepan into the sink. 'Any eggs in the house?'

Before leaving Cornwall, she had taken a course of cookery lessons, and for weeks after her arrival, his nose had twitched expectantly when he came back from the office, hoping to identify the savoury smell of roast beef. But there had been no savoury smell and no roast beef. They had sat down nightly to shredded lettuce leaves and grated nuts and other raw foods which she bought in ready-to-serve packets from the local health stores. When he staged a one-man revolution, demanding sustenance in the form of meat, he got charred chops, scorched steak and at the end of the week a butcher's bill that made him blench.

He had a bath, and then they ate, as they had so often eaten before, an omelette cooked by himself. And as always, her remorse was genuine, but not lasting; soon she was asking for details of his trip to America.

'What were you sewing?' he inquired over bread and cheese. 'And why not cut out on the table in your bedroom instead of on the floor in here?'

'My bedroom's icy. What I'm sewing is pyjamas for you—real silk, like the ones you said Oliver had. I'm cutting them out beautifully, from your old grey-and-blue striped ones. I tried a paper pattern, but it

17

wouldn't work, so I had a good idea and unpicked your old ones and—'

'You *what*?'

'Oh Rodney, don't start getting excited! All I have to do is sew them up again and—'

'The way you sewed my shirt up again, with the sleeves back to front? The way you sewed—'

'Stop *shouting*, Rodney. What's a pair of pyjamas?'

'Something to sleep in, that's all. If you had to slash up a pair, why choose the only wearable warm pair I possess? You know damned well they'll never be put together again, and all you've left me is the pair with the ruddy great slit in the leg and the collar hanging half off.'

'You've got the ones you took to America.'

'They're for wearing in boiling hot bedrooms. If I wore them here, I'd wake up a solid block of ice. Why can't you leave well alone, for God's sake?'

And why, he asked himself, digging his knife viciously into the cheese and fighting for self-control, why hadn't he left her at home, to cut up his father's pyjamas and burn his mother's saucepans? Why should he expect a man as fastidious as Oliver Tallent to look at a girl who turned her surroundings into disposal dumps?

She was watching him across the table.

'You're sorry you brought me here, aren't

18

you?' she asked slowly.

'Yes and no. What worries me is the sort of shambles your house is going to look if and when you get married. Take a look round this room. What man, what husband would stand it for more than a week?'

'I wish you'd decide exactly what you do want, Rodney,' she said. 'When I did more cleaning-up, you used to tell me I wasn't going out enough.'

'You were turning down invitations.' He was on the edge of saying that she was waiting for one from Oliver, but restrained himself. 'You can't coop yourself up.'

'Well, I'm not cooping any more. I'm more out than in. I go out with lots of men, and if you ask me, every one of them is more dreary than the last—that Osgood man and his Welsh cousin, and James Paynton and that awful Austin Bates, who's always playing practical jokes, and Ed Rogers, who's really a case; the only way I can hold him off is by dropping tranquillisers into his drinks.'

'By—?'

'Don't worry; it works. But now that we've got on to the subject of what I do with my time, I'll tell you something I was going to keep as a surprise.'

'Well?'

'I've got a job.'

He stared at her uncomprehendingly.

'Job? What job? And why?'

'Because I want one. I think if I'm out of this place all day, I'll come home from work, like you, and realise how ghastly it is, and start keeping it tidier.'

'What's the job?'

'Travel agency.'

'My God, Angela, you don't know one single thing about—'

'I don't have to know anything. All I have to do is sit there with people's tickets and meal tickets and seat reservations and bang on that little machine that clamps them together, and make them into a nice, neat booklet. Nine-thirty to five, not much money, but enough to pay for Mrs Major to come up and clean, as she used to before I came.'

'How did you hear of the job?'

'I didn't. I just thought I'd like to have one, and the nicest-looking place when I went shopping was this travel agency, so I went in and offered myself. I told them I was inexperienced, but willing to learn.'

'And they took you on?'

'Yes.'

'Then God help them.'

'There's no need to—'

'—anticipate? I suppose not. Have you told them at home?'

'Yes. I rang up the other evening. Mother was quite pleased.'

'What did the old man say?'

'He tried to be funny—like you. How was

Oliver?'

'Just the same.'

'I suppose there was a woman with him, as usual?'

'Not with him—she came in later. With flowers.'

'I know. Henrietta Gould. She makes a thing about flowers. She says she doesn't only *like* them, she *needs* them.'

'She said she'd met you.'

'She did, and went to a lot of trouble rubbing in the fact that she was moving in with Oliver. I hope she comes unstuck even faster than her predecessors. I do think he might have asked me to go and look at his new house, don't you?'

'Why does he have to invite you? You've known him all your life—why can't you ring up and ask him to show you round?'

'He'd think I was after something—and he'd be right.'

He had begun to clear away the plates, but something in her voice made him pause and study her.

'Why don't you give up?' he asked.

'I will. I practically have. Last time I ran into him, I thought, honestly I did, that he was getting dull. Not pompous, exactly, but sort of middle-aged.'

'It's time he married.'

'It won't be long now; everybody knows that Henrietta Gould's out to get him. She doesn't want to be ditched again—her last two affairs have made her feel she's beginning to skid.'

'She's not the marrying type. She runs a successful business and makes a lot of money.'

'She has to have a man around, and you wait and see: it'll be Oliver.'

'Maybe. Bring out the rest of those things, will you? I'll wash, you dry.'

'Will we ever be able to afford a machine to do it for us?'

'No. Did you look out for references to the Landini memoirs in any of the papers?'

'Yes. And cut them out for you. Everybody I meet seems to know about them.'

He nodded. Certainly everybody who was anybody in the literary world knew that D.S. Claud was going to publish them and that Oliver Tallent's agency was handling them. No longer need people crease their brows trying to identify Tallent or Laird.

'Where are you going?' Angela asked in surprise, as he went towards his room. 'Not bed so early?'

'Not to sleep. To read the Landini memoirs, as far as they've gone. If you're staying up, try not to make a clatter when you turn in, and don't leave all the lights on.'

'I forgot to tell you that the couple next door—Number 9—come in to use our phone sometimes. They haven't got theirs yet.'

'I hope they pay for the calls.'

'Yes, they do. If you're interested, their name's Grelby. He's called Peter and she's called Priss, and he's naval and she's pregnant.'

'Then you'd better warn her not to slip on Mrs Major's soap traps.'

'They asked if you could do anything to keep her in order. You're the only one she'll listen to, they said, so couldn't you talk to her and get her to—'

'No. It's no use. She hates the whole bag of newcomers, and you can't blame her. When she was young, people like them only came to districts like this when they went slumming. Now they've moved in and taken over. She's only trying to get some of her own back.'

He put on his tattered pyjamas and settled himself in bed with the Landini manuscript. He read for hours, and woke late the next morning to hear the wind howling and dashing spatters of rain against his window. He put on a dressing-gown and slippers and went into the living room. Angela was out, but she had tidied up, according to her lights: the work-basket and the snippets of material had been pushed under a chair and his cut-up pyjamas and a length of silk were spread on the sofa. She had left his breakfast ready: a coffee pot on a heater whose flame had been turned up too high, a loaf of bread, an electric toaster and a jar of the glutinous lumps of orange peel she called home-made marmalade. He fetched milk and butter from the refrigerator, wondering, as he left the ice-cold kitchen, why they needed one.

He sat down to eat, the morning paper

23

propped in front of him. The coffee was little more than dregs, but nothing could take from him the feeling of being at home, at peace. He was grateful for a long, lazy morning during which he could recall the interest and enjoyment with which he had read the memoirs the night before. He wanted to pick up the telephone and discuss them with Oliver, but there would be time enough when he went to the office after lunch. In the meantime, he scanned the headlines and decided that life wasn't at all bad. The Landini memoirs had revived the moribund firm of D.S. Claud. Business was looking up, though the fact would probably not have much effect on his salary. On the personal side, he was grateful for a healthy body and a face that could not be called worse than plain, grateful to Mrs Major for refusing to sell the house. Life was good, and Madame Landini's memoirs were magnificent.

He heard Angela's footsteps on the stairs; she came in carrying a string bag swollen with purchases. Her mackintosh dripped as she crossed to the kitchen.

He got up and made more coffee, and she sat down to have a second breakfast.

'Filthy day, and I had to put petrol in your car,' she told him. 'You owe me a pound and eighty pence. I didn't know whether you'd be going into the office today, so I put it back in the garage.' She cut more bread. 'This is nice, having you for breakfast. Like Sunday. Are you going to take the day off?'

'No. I want to talk to Oliver. And I want to start on some of the work that Claudius has undoubtedly been piling up on my desk while I've been away.'

'Your light was on for hours. Did you finish the memoirs?'

'As far as they go, yes.'

'How far's that?'

'About halfway. She's just finished the account of her husband's disappearance.'

'Landini disappeared?'

'Not Landini. Her first husband, who was also her accompanist. Name of Anton Veitch.'

'Where did he disappear to?'

'Overboard. Oddly enough, Father, then a sub-lieutenant, was on one of the ships that searched for him.'

'Father? My father?'

'And mine. Funny assignment for the Royal Navy, cruising round looking for an accompanist. But he was rather a special accompanist.'

'Did they find him?'

'No.'

'Did he fall overboard, or did someone push him?'

'Who'd push him? He was a nice fellow, from all accounts. He started off as a concert pianist—brilliant, they said—but gave it up to marry her.'

25

'How long had they been married before he fell overboard?'

'Eight years.'

'Long enough for her to get tired of him.'

'She wasn't tired of him. They—'

He stopped at the sound of the telephone, and went across the room and lifted the receiver. He heard Oliver's voice; seconds later, his mood of contentment was shattered.

'Rodney? Can you meet me at your office? Something's come up.'

'What's wrong?'

'She's called it off.'

'She's . . . she's *what?*'

'The memoirs. She's not going on with them.'

'She can't. I mean, she must. She's got to. My God, she can't—'

'She has. I rang your office to find out if you were there, and got Claudius, and he gave me the news. He's waiting for us. I'm going there now.'

'Have you—' Rodney began, and stopped; the line was dead. He replaced the receiver with a crash and made for his room.

'Bad news?' Angela asked anxiously as he passed her.

'Madame Landini.'

'Dead?'

'Worse. Halted in midstream.' He was in his room. 'Go and bring the car round, will you? That'll save a bit of time.'

26

CHAPTER TWO

He drove as fast as he could through the rain-washed streets—but at this hour, traffic was at its heaviest and vehicles crawled nose to tail, seldom offering a space which he could seize. He did as much thrusting as he could; once he received an impression, strengthened by the remarks of the driver, that he had plunged under the rear of a bus and emerged at the front. As he drove, a part of his mind ranged over the history—which looked like being a brief history—of his association with Madame Landini and her memoirs.

It was through him that the book had come to the firm of D.S. Claud. It had seemed to him at the time a matter of pure chance, but further acquaintance with Madame Landini had made him realise that in her affairs, not much was left to chance.

Yet chance had begun it all. On a fine morning last September, he had left the office to keep a business appointment in Knightsbridge. He had not used his car; he had gone by bus and decided to return on foot, giving himself some exercise in the Park on the way. He was walking briskly beside the Serpentine when his musing was interrupted by the sound of a dog fight; a short distance ahead, a bellicose Alsatian was attempting to

27

make a meal of a miniature poodle. The poodle's owner, an elderly lady, had with more courage than sense snatched the little animal up into her arms and was doing her best to protect it from assault.

Rodney looked round in the hope of seeing a hero or two speeding to the rescue—but there was only himself. He broke into a run, reached the scene and by seizing the Alsatian in places as far removed from its teeth as possible, managed to drag it to the water's edge, and dunked the struggling mass of fur. Then he turned to the lady, to find her shaken and dishevelled; the damage to the poodle was a torn ear. Steering them towards the exit and a taxi, he realised that he himself was being steered towards a waiting Rolls-Royce manned by a chauffeur, who at sight of his mistress came hurrying to assist her. Rodney considered his part to be at an end, but was begged by the lady to escort her to her home. He was not surprised to learn that it was in Park Lane, for he had by now identified her: she was Madame Landini, born a Russian princess, in her youth and middle years a concert singer of international fame, now the widow of one of the richest men in Europe and still of sufficient interest to reporters to make her name and appearance familiar to the present-day public.

There was no conversation on the drive to the house; Madame Landini leaned against the cushions with her eyes closed, while Rodney held the poodle and mopped its ear with his handkerchief. On arrival, he handed Madame Landini out, gave her into the care of a capable-looking butler and accepted the offer of the car to drive him to his office. The incident was reported in the evening papers, the account stating that Madame Landini had been attacked by a dog and rescued by a gentleman named Robert Aird, who did not give his address.

Ten days passed. Rodney had almost forgotten the matter, when a letter was delivered by hand to the office: Madame Landini wished to give herself the pleasure of receiving Mr Laird to tea on Thursday at five o'clock.

He arrived punctually, was admitted, relieved of his wet mackintosh and conducted along broad, thickly-carpeted corridors. A double door was opened, his name was intoned and he found himself in a vast drawing room whose temperature he reckoned to be in the mid-eighties. By the fireplace stood Madame Landini, one arm resting on the elaborate overmantle—a stately, studied attitude well suited to her long, draped, sea-green gown. He made his way to her, bowed over her hand in what he hoped was polished style, and was invited to be seated.

Her opening speech expressed gratitude— such courage, such coolness, such strength!

Yes, thank you, the little poodle was recovering, it had been sent for recuperation to kennels in the country, she had taken it for a walk that morning never for a moment suspecting that it was in a condition in which it should be kept from gentlemen dogs. But for the intervention of God and His instrument—Mr Laird—what would have happened?

Before the point could be debated, the door opened to admit two footmen and a tea trolley which looked to Rodney the size of a ping-pong table. On it he saw a snowy cloth, several pieces of beautiful Georgian silver, delicate cups and saucers, cress sandwiches, wafer-thin brown bread and butter, hot scones in a covered silver dish, and a variety of cakes and biscuits. There were three cups, and he heard Madame Landini ordering one of the footmen to convey her compliments to Signor Piozzi. Signor Piozzi, entering a few minutes later, proved to be short, stout and grey-haired, with an alert expression and small, extremely shrewd black-button eyes. He was, Madame Landini told Rodney, a financial genius, for over thirty years man of business to her friend the Maharajah of Hardanipur, temporarily on loan to herself to advise in the sale to His Highness of some property she owned in Italy. Signor Piozzi entered the conversation in machine-gun Italian, found that Rodney knew none and with unconcealed annoyance switched to English. He ate and drank nothing. Madame took tea with a slice of lemon. Rodney accepted a biscuit, discovering too late that it was a crackly one which made him sound like a horse scrunching oats. Prevented for a time from conversing, he fell to wondering why the name Hardanipur sounded familiar. In the recesses of his mind, a faint bell had rung. Hardanipur...

The trolley was wheeled out, Signor Piozzi rose, bowed and beat a brisk retreat. Rodney glanced at his watch and decided that another twenty minutes was as much as etiquette required, or that he could endure. All he need do was stay awake and listen to Madame Landini and try to look interested.

Listening, he confirmed his impression that on her social chessboard there were no pawns, but a disproportionate number of kings and queens. Also mentioned were some oriental rulers and eastern despots, all old and dear friends, the oldest and dearest being the Maharajah she had previously mentioned. He had, Madame said, been living for many years in Switzerland.

'You know, he has not been back to India since the British handed over power. He left everything—his palaces, his possessions, his elephants, his thousand servants, his fleets of limousines. Dispossessed, Mr Laird; this is a link between us. I, too, am an exile from the land of my birth.'

31

Overheated, bored, drowsy as he was, Rodney nevertheless came sharply to attention five minutes later, when he detected in Madame's tone a sudden, subtle change, a fractional change of key that had become familiar to him since first he had begun to have dealings with authors. Meeting them for lunch, he nowadays found it interesting to speculate at what stage in the meal the new note would sound. It might come between the cheese and the coffee; it might even come with the *osso bucco*; in the case of women writers, it sometimes sounded as early as the soup—but come it inevitably did, this difference that marked the leap from borsch to business, from ravioli to royalties. His eyes, fixed on Madame Landini, showed for a moment surprise and a gleam of expectancy: a proposition was on the way.

She presented it in businesslike fashion. She had decided, she said, to write her memoirs. People had for some time past been urging her to do so, pointing out the rich treasures of musical, of social, even of political history that would pour from her pen. But she had hesitated because she could not face the side issues, those small, tiresome details that came between an artist and his work, details from which during her career as a singer she had been carefully shielded. She had no wish to entangle herself in a net of agreements, contracts, time schedules. She had almost put aside the project—and then? How extraordinary that out of nowhere had come someone who, besides proving himself a man of courage and delicacy, had also proved to be a member of a publishing firm, someone to whom she could with confidence confide her memoirs, who would undertake to leave her free to devote herself to writing, while he would … Here she paused, as the authors paused, leaving the words 'hand over the money' hanging in the air.

He had no doubt that she was shrewd enough to have informed herself of the state as well as the status of the firm. She would have learned that it was reputable, and she probably believed—as he did—that the book would carry its own weight of success. He was aware, before she had finished speaking, that it would act as a blood-transfusion for D.S. Claud—and he would see to it that she became Oliver Tallent's client.

When she ended, he heard himself promising to put the proposal before Mr Claud. He even made a proviso: that she submit the manuscript to him in instalments. This had been a safety measure, for he had no proof that she could write. He had learned that she could.

She had written half the book—and now refused to go on.

*   *   *

Oliver was waiting for him in his room at the office.

'This is how it goes,' he said at once. 'You remember the secretary I mentioned last night, the one I engaged for Madame Landini? She had instructions to come to this office every Friday on her way home, to get her salary. Claudius's accountant paid her. Yesterday, she asked to see Claudius, but he'd left, so she told her story to the accountant, old Armstrong, and asked him to pass it on.'

'What went wrong?'

'She didn't know. Everything had been going smoothly—no sign of trouble anywhere. Before leaving last night, she took some typed sheets into Madame's room; Madame looked over them for corrections, said they didn't need any, and added a few friendly words. The girl—I can't remember her name—'

'Baird.'

'That's right, Baird. She got ready to leave, went out of her room—and ran straight into Madame, who was apparently having hysterics. She shouted—yelled, this girl said—tore the last sheets of the manuscript into shreds and hurled them over the banisters, and then told the girl to get out and stay out. That's the story Claudius was told when he arrived this morning. He put a call through to Madame Landini at once, of course, but she's speaking to nobody.'

'Who answered the phone?'

34

'A voice which summoned another voice which said that the doctor had forbidden any communication whatsoever. Claudius is waiting for us. Let's go.'

They walked together down the narrow, uncarpeted corridor, and Rodney opened a door and ushered Oliver into a large room overlooking the street. From behind the desk a thin, stooping, grey-haired man greeted them: D.S. Claud the fourth.

The firm had been in existence since 1825. The first D.S. Claud, known as Claudius One, had been a country squire with an ample fortune and a splendid estate in Surrey. Casting about for a gentlemanly pursuit with which to occupy some of his leisure hours, he hit on publishing, and rented as business premises a double-storied building not far from Fleet Street. Here he spent the weekday mornings, the afternoons being devoted to the search for medieval suits of armour, of which he had a notable collection.

His successor, Claudius Two, limited his office mornings to three a week, thus giving himself time to add to his collection of musicians' marble busts. The available space in the Surrey mansion being taken up by the suits of armour, the busts were displayed in the office.

Claudius Three was a well-known and popular sportsman who dropped into the office when not prevented by hunting, shooting or fishing. He collected nothing but debts; thus when Claudius Four emerged unscathed from the Second World War, he found himself the possessor of a gratuity, a mortgaged mansion, a moribund publishing firm, eighty busts and sixty suits of armour. He also had a widowed sister named Phoebe, who was even poorer than himself. Together they sold the mansion and the suits of armour, decided to leave the busts where they were, bought two copies of a publication entitled *The Ins and Outs of Publishing* and went to work, sustained by the hope that the firm's assets, and the lease of the building, would last as long as they themselves were likely to.

Claudius Four worked in the room overlooking the street because it was the only view left to him, the low buildings to right and left having been demolished by enemy bombs and giant structures of steel erected in their place. From behind his desk, Chopin and Liszt stared sightlessly across the room at Bach and Beethoven.

Phoebe, though a widow, had from the beginning of her reign at the office been known as Miss Phoebe. She was, or had been until Rodney's arrival, the firm's mainstay and prop. Immensely forceful, she was to her timid brother part bulwark, part bugler sounding the Charge. She acted as extra secretary to both Claudius and Rodney, but her chief usefulness lay in her ability to handle even the most

36

troublesome of authors; she quelled the grumblers and put down the high and mighty. In times of storm, her policy was one of waiting for passions to cool; this she called turning down the gas. Taking authors out to lunch she left to her brother and to Rodney, she herself preparing a snack in a small room which had been fitted up as a kitchen. Childless, she looked on Rodney as a son, but regarded Oliver with jealous suspicion, well knowing that he had done his best and intermittently was still doing his best to persuade Rodney to become his partner.

On his entry with Oliver, Rodney received a warm welcome, delivered in Claudius's soft, gentle, musical voice.

'It's nice to have you back, Rodney. Sit down. Sit down, both of you. Rodney, this is not a happy return for you, I fear.'

After his month's absence, Rodney thought the old man looked shrunken. As usual, he was sitting with a pair of glasses pushed to the end of his nose, the tips of his fingers together, leaning forward in an attitude so reminiscent of a medical practitioner that authors at their first interview found themselves discussing symptoms instead of stories. Never had Rodney felt more strongly that fate had played a mean trick in creating a man for a quiet, country setting and then placing him behind a City desk. Claudius should be pottering about among his rose beds, not rallying his forces to face a literary crisis.

'We won't take up time now talking about your trip, Rodney,' he said. 'I think we ought to discuss first—don't you?—this business of Madame Landini and her ... shall we call it an attack of temperament?'

'You think it's merely temperament?' Oliver inquired.

'It's only a guess, a mere guess. I tried several times this morning to reach her by telephone, but the answer was always the same: Madame is ill, and can't see or speak to anybody. But her display ... what else can it be called but temperament? We must bear in mind that she is a great artist, and they say that artists are ruled by their temperaments. Mind you, I'm only putting this forward as a ... well, as a suggestion.'

'She's been working hard,' Oliver commented. 'She's probably overworked.'

'Overworked at what?' Rodney demanded. 'All she's had to do for the past month was sit on a sofa and dictate her memoirs to a secretary.'

'Such a pity, such a great pity that I wasn't in the office when she came here last evening,' Claudius murmured. 'Perhaps I could have found out what occurred—but the only person left was Mr Armstrong, and she gave him very few details. Then he paid her salary, and she went away. There must be a great deal more that she didn't say. We have her address. I feel,

Rodney, that you, or Oliver, or both of you should get hold of her and bring her here, or find out from her exactly what took place. Mind you, this is a mere suggestion...'

'She was sacked,' Oliver said. 'That's what took place.'

'But why? That's what we've got to find out. Rodney, can you think of any reason why Madame Landini should have decided not to go on?'

Rodney saw Oliver's eyes on him, and guessed what was in his mind; he had never believed that Madame Landini had taken the precaution of making inquiries about the firm before offering the book to Rodney. Now, he seemed to be saying, Madame had decided that the firm hadn't enough prestige. If that were the case, Rodney thought with sudden fury, then let her take her book to the devil.

His eyes rested on the spare figure behind the desk, and no illusion clouded his gaze. He knew that Claudius was inefficient and ineffectual and hopelessly behind the times—but he loved him. No words could express what he felt for the firm of D.S. Claud when on a morning in Cornwall more than three years ago he had read their letter and then gone down to the sea's edge to read it again. Those moments of exaltation, exultation, that time of pure, heady elation he owed to Claudius and Phoebe, who had written—after it had been refused by fifteen publishers—to tell him that they would accept his novel. Nothing—not his knowledge that the book was not worth printing, not his realisation that he no longer wanted to be a writer; not even his belief, later confirmed, that when published it would prove a total loss—nothing could ever take from him or erase from his memory those glorious moments with surf singing in his ears and gulls wheeling round him as he stood with the letter in his hand. When he joined the firm instead of joining Oliver, he felt that he had paid part of his debt; bringing the firm the Landini memoirs had perhaps paid off the rest.

He heard Oliver speaking.

'It did strike me'—the deep, precise tones contrasted strongly with Claudius's gentle, hesitant speech—'that this might be Madame Landini's way of getting you to offer her a higher scale of royalties. We've learned that she's a first-class writer—which we didn't know when the contract was drawn up. I haven't asked you what you think of the book as far as it's gone, but—'

'Oh, it's splendid, splendid. Without any doubt. It's magnificent. Especially her early life. I was carried away, absolutely carried away by the description of her childhood and her parents and her link with that unfortunate royal family. And the flight to Paris was extremely well told, and their poverty ... yes, I was carried away, there's no other way of expressing it. Surely you're not of the opinion,

40

Oliver, that having got so far, having relived those days, Madame Landini is going to stoop to bargaining for better terms?'

'It's a possibility.'

'No,' Rodney said with conviction. 'If that's what she was after, she would have sent for me and told me so. What's far more likely is that the last chapter or two upset her—recalling and recording her first husband's end. She broke off just after his death. That, if you like, could account for her getting into a nervous state. It was a pretty shattering experience. I thought her description of her feelings was pretty moving.'

'Ahem, yes.' Claudius gave a nervous cough. 'But there's just one point I would mention in that connection. The description contained some, er, some inaccuracies.'

The two younger men stared at him in astonishment.

'I don't quite understand,' Oliver said. 'Do you mean that her account doesn't tie up with what the newspapers said at the time?'

'Oh, no, no, no. I am speaking from my, so to speak, inside knowledge, which I got from a letter which was written to me at the time, by a person who travelled on the ship with Madame Landini.'

'On the *Atlantis*?' Rodney asked.

'Yes. On the *Atlantis*.'

There was a pause.

'You haven't mentioned this before,' Oliver said.

41

'No. That is ... no. You see, it was like this: Before mentioning the ... we can perhaps call it the coincidence, I felt I would like to wait and see exactly how Madame Landini would write about it—or indeed, if she would write about it at all, that's to say about it in any great detail. It was, as we all know after reading the memoirs, and as Rodney has just pointed out, a very difficult time for her. Very difficult indeed. It struck me that what she wrote about it might offer a guide to the general frankness, the general accuracy of the book. Perhaps you don't quite follow me. I'm trying to say that it is impossible for any of us to know, to guess, to gauge the exact amount of truth, of unclouded truth there is in any personal account of this kind. The question has been in my mind before, when we've published memoirs—none, of course, to be compared with Madame Landini's. In those other cases, I had no means of placing what I knew against what was written. This time, I had. Knowing what I knew about the circumstances of Madame's first husband's death, I allowed myself ... Do I make myself clear?'

'What did she have to hide?' Oliver asked. 'There were no failures to be recorded or conveniently forgotten, no humiliations she'd want to gloss over. Why did you think she wouldn't be frank about Anton Veitch's death?'

'Because it was the only incident in her entire

42

career that held any element of mystery. You two are young men; you have no idea of the sensation the event made when it happened. I have. What is more, I knew exactly what had happened. I wanted to wait and see what Madame Landini's version was. I have now read it, and I find that it contradicts certain facts which I happen to know are true facts.'

Rodney pulled his chair closer to the desk.

'Begin at the beginning,' he requested. 'Did you sail on the *Atlantis* on that voyage?'

'No. I must explain first that my sister and I had at that time succeeded in selling my grandfather's collection of medieval suits of armour to an American named Mr Harding. I went down to Southampton to say goodbye to him and check that all the crates had been put safely on board. There was a little time left before the ship sailed, so while Mrs Harding was taken by an official to see Madame Landini's—that's to say, Princess Anna's—private suite, Mr Harding and I sat in a kind of glassed-in bar on the deck and ordered a drink.'

He paused, took off his glasses and placed them on the desk; he needed no glasses to see into the past. He sat staring at his large, unblemished leather blotter, and at last Rodney prompted him.

'You ordered a drink...'

'Yes. And as we sat there, we saw the Princess come aboard—the Princess and her

43

entourage. She was more beautiful than I can say. I had seen her on the concert platform, but never as close as I was seeing her then. You can have no idea, or very little, as you look at her today, what a glorious creature she was. She...' Claudius cleared his throat. 'Well, she went to stand at the rail, to wave to the crowd that had gathered on the dock to see her. Her husband was beside her, and they made a well-matched pair; he was as striking, in his way, as she was in hers. She was standing in a sea of flowers—sheaves in her arms, baskets surrounding her. At the moment that Mr Harding decided that it was time he went to look for his wife, the signal was given for non-travellers to leave the ship. The Princess's husband, Anton Veitch, leaned towards her and spoke a few words—as you know from her memoirs, it was his invariable habit, when they travelled, to make certain that all arrangements had been made for her comfort, and he was going down to their stateroom to make his usual check. He picked up as many of the floral tributes as he could hold, to take with him, and he passed close to me. As he went by, our glances met for a moment, and we both smiled at the rather absurd picture he made. I always think it so extraordinary that I must have been almost the last person who saw him alive; certainly nobody else ever claimed to have seen him after he left the deck. You've read the rest of it. When the Princess eventually

44

went down to her suite, the flowers were there. Their luggage had been unpacked. The ship was moving down the Solent. When her husband failed to join her, she gave the matter no thought; even when the ship was out in the Channel and the dinner menu was brought to her stateroom, she felt no anxiety; he might be with the other members of her party, he might be in the bar, he might be anywhere.'

Once again he paused, once again Rodney prompted.

'So we come to the letter you mentioned,' he said.

'Yes. The letter. What Madame Landini wrote in the manuscript is that when her husband failed to appear, she was distraught. Her own word: distraught. She writes, and writes superbly, of the growing uneasiness, the mounting tension, the search from one end of the ship to the other, the word going round: Anton Veitch was overboard. The ship stopped, a lifeboat lowered, a crowd of passengers gathered outside the Princess's suite. Among them were Mr and Mrs Harding. They were all asked to move away, but the Hardings' stateroom was next to the Princess's suite, and they heard much of what went on. Mr Harding wrote to me as soon as he reached New York—so that events were still fresh in his mind, and what he wrote was that the Princess was not so much distraught as enraged. He said she sounded like an animal deprived of its prey.

He used the word baulked. He went on to say, to write, that he thought it was the first time the Princess had ever found herself in a situation in which her feelings weren't the primary consideration. In her memoirs, she says that she paced the deck all night. Mr Harding wrote, and I believe him, that she was given a strong sedative which kept her quiet until the ship reached New York; then she was carried ashore, as she states, and her concerts were cancelled and so on. I am merely trying to point out that in Mr Harding's view, her rage against Fate was stronger than her grief. That being so, I cannot agree that writing about the event would result in her having this breakdown, or whatever you choose to call it.'

'She doesn't have to reveal all her feelings in her memoirs, does she?' Rodney asked.

'She may reveal them or she may conceal them,' Claudius said. 'What she should not do is fabricate them. I still have the letter from Mr Harding. It was a business letter and contained a cheque—the balance of what he owed me. You may see it at any time, if you want to.'

'Was there any speculation, in the press or in rumours at the time, that Veitch had any reason to go overboard?' Oliver asked.

'My dear Oliver'—Claudius spoke protestingly—'why should he have wanted to give up what most men spend their lives trying to win: beauty, wealth, fame?'

'Her fame. Not his fame,' Rodney pointed

out. 'He'd given up his own career to become her accompanist.'

'If he wanted to get away from her, why embark on the journey?' Claudius asked. 'I was merely challenging Madame Landini's description of her state of mind. I don't question the fact that his disappearance was pure misadventure. He isn't the first person who has leaned too far over a ship's rail, and I'm afraid he won't be the last. But we've strayed rather far from the real point of this meeting; shall we get back to it? Will one of you go and see this girl?'

'You,' Oliver told Rodney.

Rodney rose. 'All right. What's her address?'

'Mr Armstrong will give it to you,' Claudius said. 'No telephone number, unfortunately; he didn't think of asking.'

Rodney went to his room to get his coat. In the corridor, he came face to face with Miss Phoebe, who was coming out of her room. Their faces were almost on a level, for she was very tall. She was also gaunt, with a severe aspect that was useful in cowing teenage typists.

She offered a cheek to Rodney and he kissed it, being careful not to dislodge her hat. Nobody in the office had ever seen her without it—a black felt, unrelieved in winter, in spring decorated with young leaves, in summer beribboned, in autumn hung with bunches of

47

artificial fruit. Her suits were like her hat—plain, black and seasonally enlivened. Her voice, which she tried in vain to lower when discussing confidential matters, boomed down the corridors and echoed through all the rooms.

'Nice to have you back,' she told him. 'We missed you. Before you embark on a travelogue, tell me what's behind this story that's buzzing round the office. They've only just thought of mentioning it to me. About Madame Landini. What's going on?'

He told her, and explained that he was on his way to get the secretary's address.

'You needn't bother Mr Armstrong,' she said. 'I made a note of it in one of your files when we engaged her. I'll show you.'

She led the way to his room and produced it, and he took his coat from the peg in a corner of the room.

'You'll also see there on your desk,' she told him, 'a note you can deal with when you get back. Luncheon engagement. I've entered it in your diary too. The fourteenth. I'll remind you, because if I don't, you'll try to get out of it.'

He glanced at the note.

'No,' he said firmly.

'Yes,' Phoebe said with equal firmness. 'You had no business to fob her off on to my brother last time. You saw the state she reduced him to. You're getting very foxy at leaving all the

48

troublesome cases to poor Claudius. Has he told you the story of seeing Mr Harding off on the *Atlantis*?'

'Yes.'

'It doesn't prove anything that I can see. If you're writing about your life, you put in what you like and keep out what you like, as I told him. Why do you have to chase after this girl?'

'I told you—we want her story of what happened.'

'Great waste of time. It's not likely, is it, that a storm like that could have been raised by anything that a recently-installed secretary said or did? It's far more likely to be a financial crisis of some kind—isn't that Italian accountant staying with Madame Landini to arrange some deal or other?'

'She's selling some property in Italy, to the Maharajah of Hardanipur. The name rings a bell, but I don't know where I heard it.'

'You wouldn't need to have heard it. You may have seen it. He's often in the news. He lives in Switzerland and throws millions around in a careless fashion. Isn't that Italian accountant called Piozzi?'

'Yes.'

'The Maharajah took him over when Landini died. Piozzi's function is to look for legal loopholes and slide gracefully through them. I'm not an accountant's widow for nothing; I had to sit through many a dreary dinner listening to my husband and his friends

49

discussing deals. Piozzi's never acted for anybody but Landini and this Maharajah. It all came back to me the other day when I read the reference to him in Madame's memoirs—you remember she went on a trip to India with her first husband, and stayed with the Maharajah in royal state?'

'She told me he left everything—'

'So he did. Everything but his millions and his diamonds. But we're wasting time. What were we talking about before . . . Oh, that girl. I don't see what's to be gained by your going to see her. Far better to give the thing time to settle. That's what I would have advised if I'd come in this morning in time to attend that three-cornered meeting you and Oliver and my brother were holding. I would have counselled waiting.'

'Yes, I know. Turn down the gas.'

'Certainly, and then the pot won't boil over. You have to meet temperament with patience and calm—when am I going to succeed in teaching you that? You have to learn the technique of banking down the fires. For example, if people shout at you, what you must do is say you're sorry, but you didn't quite catch. That means they have to shout it all over again, and by the time they've had to do that several times, the grievance has lost its force. Let Madame simmer for a few days.'

Rodney patted her shoulder.

'Excellent advice,' he said. 'I'll make a note of it. But now I've got to carry out the boss's orders. See you later.'

He left the office and walked to his car; getting in, he glanced at the paper on which Phoebe had written the secretary's address, and found to his annoyance that it was in a district well beyond Pimlico—in this traffic, it would take him nearly an hour to get there. When he did, he was further annoyed to find that he had insufficiently studied the spidery scrawl before leaving the office; it could be Alderman Place, Alderman Grove, Alderman Terrace or Alderman Street, all of which radiated from Alderman Square. He tried Number 15 in the Place, the Grove, the Terrace and the Square; nothing now remained but the Street. He mounted the steps of a dreary-looking house with crumbling brickwork, an open front door and an inner hall decorated with innumerable cards pinned to a board or stuck on the walls. He went twice along the line, but found nothing to indicate that Miss Nicola Baird lived there. He went outside again and pressed long and insistently a bell marked *Caretaker*. After an interval, he heard a sound below him and looked down to see a woman with a towel round her head leaning out of a basement window and pointing to the area steps, to indicate that he should descend. Descending, he found her waiting for him in a narrow doorway.

'Come in, quick,' she ordered. 'I'll catch my death.'

As well as the towel, she was wearing slippers, a striped blouse and tight trousers over which was tied a grease-spattered apron. She had a heavy cold, and when Rodney entered a kitchen almost as cold as his own, he saw on the table a basin from which rose steam and a strong odour of balsam. She bent over it and spoke from under the towel.

'No wooms bacant, sobby.'

'I'm not after a room,' Rodney told her. 'I'm looking for a Miss Baird.'

'Bom.'

'Gone?'

'Ah. Bom this borning.'

'I see. Do you happen to know where she went?'

'Hob.'

'Home?'

She emerged from under the towel and through streaming eyes glared at him.

'I told you—she went this morning. She gave up her room, and that suited me because somebody was waiting for it.'

'Didn't she leave an address?'

'Of course she left an address. How would you expect her to get her letters sent on, if she didn't leave an address? I've got it somewhere, but I can't look now. I can't let this steam go off. Come back in ten minutes.'

Her head disappeared under the towel, and he thought it useless to argue; he went out, bought a newspaper and sat in the car. When fifteen minutes had elapsed, he made his way once more down the area steps. Given permission to enter, he went in and found the woman opening drawer after drawer, turning over crumpled papers and muttering curses. Banging the last drawer shut, she turned her steam-flushed face to Rodney and was about to speak when her eyes fell on a piece of paper protruding from a vase. She snatched it.

'There's the blasted thing,' she said. 'Here you are. Shut the door quick when you go.'

He drove to Oliver's office and gave him a brief report.

'That's her home address in Brighton—we already had it,' Oliver told him. 'Pity you went to all that trouble for nothing.'

'As well as catching that woman's cold, probably. Do you think it's worth pursuing?'

'Yes. Don't you?'

'No. The girl's told her story. If she was involved, if the row had anything to do with her, if it was something she said or did to make Madame Landini break into hysterics, she's not likely to admit it, is she? What do you expect her to say that she didn't say to old Armstrong yesterday?'

'Nothing—but all we've got is a second-hand account. The girl's efficient and, I'd say, observant. You could ask questions and find out—'

'Why don't you go down?'

'This is your pigeon. I would have thought you'd be only too keen to get a detailed account of what happened.'

'I'd much rather see Madame Landini—if they'd let me. In fact, that's what I'll try first. If I don't get in, I'll go down to Brighton. Tomorrow. And I only hope it won't prove a damned waste of a day.' He paused, staring moodily at the desk. 'Have you considered the kind of fools we'll look if she really has come to a halt?'

'We'll be where we were before.'

'That's right—we will. You'll go back to acting for authors anonymous, and poor old Claudius will lose the chance to retire with dignity. Apart from those two considerations, we'll lose a book that might have been the success of the century. It's a history of our times, told by a woman who was born in a golden aura and kept it round her all her life. Princess, petted by the Tsar. Paris, and the Russian nobility on their beam ends. A consummate artist dedicated to her art. A revolution and two world wars. Kings and princes as lovers, and every lover a lever to raise her higher in her profession, which wasn't the profession it would have been if she'd been a lesser or a less gifted woman. A foreground of glittering success—once her career got under way—and in the background, like a drumbeat, work, work, work, work. She ... Damn it, are you listening?'

'I was. I told you some time back that I agreed with every word, but you didn't hear me. I never really knew what a publisher's blurb was; thank you.'

Rodney began to speak, broke off in disgust and went out to his car. He drove to Park Lane; if Madame Landini was unable to see him, he would be no worse off. If they let him in, he might learn enough to save him the trip to Brighton.

To his surprise, he was admitted, but his initial feeling of relief drained slowly away as he followed a footman down corridors far narrower, far less luxuriously carpeted than those which on his first visit had led to the drawing room. He was ushered into a small ground-floor room and left to wait; looking round him, he saw a desk on which stood a typewriter and files, while near by were neat shelves of reference books and a filing cabinet. He realised that this was the room in which Miss Baird of Brighton had worked.

The door opened, and he turned, half expecting to be told that nobody, after all, could see him. But it was not a servant who entered.

Rodney could not afterwards assess how many seconds passed before he regained his wits. The figure standing before him needed no identification. From the top of his beautifully-shaped head, down his large, powerful body to his elegantly-shod feet, a prince. A prince—whether ruling or dispossessed made no matter. He felt pleasure and admiration, and also gratitude to Nature, who made so many lamentable mistakes, but who this time had achieved a perfect piece of casting. Immense, but every ounce carried with ease and grace. Clear olive skin, a strong jaw, large, long-lashed dark eyes that looked in lazy amusement at the world. If a man of—what? sixty-five?—could be called beautiful, then here, Rodney thought, was the man.

He was wearing a coat of natural-coloured brocade which fitted closely round his neck and ended in a flare at the knees. His trousers were of heavy silk, cut in jodhpur pattern, tight at knee and ankle. His feet were thrust into soft brown calf slippers. He glanced round the room, and the gleam of amusement in his eyes died and gave place to a look which suggested that scimitars were flashing through the air.

'Mr Laird, please accept my apology on Madame's behalf. You should not have been shown into this room. You must forgive us; the household is rather disorganised.'

If you closed your eyes, Rodney thought, an Englishman was speaking. He pulled himself together.

'Your Highness, I came to—'

'You have come to make inquiries about

Madame; of course. Be seated, please. I arrived last night, to find that Madame had been ordered to rest. The doctor will allow her to see me, but nobody else. Perhaps she has told you that I am one of her oldest and closest friends?'

'Yes, sir; she did. Do you think that writing her memoirs has exhausted, has been too much for her?'

'Emotionally, yes. I'll confess something: when she showed me what she'd written, I was ... amazed is too mild a term; I was astounded. Since the death of her first husband, Anton Veitch, she has hardly mentioned his name—and those of us who know her well have seldom ventured to speak of him. So when I read the details she had given of his end ... I found it incredible. I've absolutely no doubt that writing about him is what brought on this breakdown. I can't be too thankful that I chose this moment to arrive.'

'Speaking professionally, sir, I suppose I can derive comfort from the fact that the painful account is now behind her, and not ahead?'

'You mean that the worst is over, and she'll now recover and go on with her memoirs?'

'I hope so.'

'For your sake, I hope so too. But nobody is going to be allowed to mention the word memoirs to her until the doctor lifts his ban. My own feeling, if you won't mind my telling you this, is that she should never have been persuaded to embark on the project.'

57

'The proposal didn't come from us, sir; it came from Madame,' Rodney said, and saw an instant's surprise on the Maharajah's face.

'But Madame told me—' he began, and stopped. 'All I know, Mr Laird, is that the doctor says she must be kept quite quiet. I promise to tell you if there's any change.' He went to the desk. 'Would you write down your telephone number? Your office number is here, but I'd like to have your private number, so that I can send you a message if the doctor says that Madame can see you.'

Rodney wrote down the number and straightened to find the Maharajah regarding him with amusement.

'You, of course, are the hero of the Alsatian encounter,' he said. 'I've only just made the connection. She wrote and told me about it at the time, but I didn't picture you as you are.'

Rodney smiled. 'A rather homely hero, sir?'

'A hero who seems to know how to handle Madame. Isn't this the very first crisis since she embarked on the memoirs?'

'Yes.'

'You're fortunate. I'm sure there'll be others. Madame doesn't create situations— they simply build up round her. Her visit to me with her first husband brought the fact home to me. You'll probably grow to admire her as much as I do, but no association with her can be crisis-free.'

'Will you be staying long, sir?'

'I shall certainly stay until Madame has recovered. I may have to do one or two business trips, but they'll be brief. I hope we shall meet again.'

Rodney took his leave. The bow which practice had made perfect seemed to him inadequate on this occasion; he thought it would be more fitting if he folded up in front of the brown calf slippers, and buried a respectful nose in the rug. The Maharajah did not ring to have him shown out; he accompanied him— perhaps, Rodney thought, to see that he didn't make a sudden leap towards the stairs and Madame's bedroom. His manner was relaxed and friendly; strolling along the corridors, they discussed Geneva, where the Maharajah was living, and Venice, to which he would move when his arrangements for the purchase of Madame Landini's palace were completed.

'There is one more angle to consider, Mr Laird,' he said, pausing as they neared the entrance hall. 'Don't imagine for a moment that these business negotiations have exhausted Madame.' He threw back his head and gave a deep bark of amusement. 'Madame and I both have a method by which we avoid fatigue over financial matters. The method is called Guido Piozzi. All we are required to do is sign our names on the place to which he points.'

Several functionaries had gathered to show Rodney out, but the Maharajah came to the door before halting to make his apologies.

'I shall leave you here, Mr Laird. These clothes'—he made a gesture that took in the long brocade coat and silk trousers—'are purely for indoor wear. When I go out, I look like everybody else.'

Rodney met the dark, amused eyes.

'A pity, sir,' he commented, and walked down the steps and to his car. Park Lane looked new and strange; when had buses superseded richly-caparisoned elephants? And now that he was hobnobbing with Maharajahs, shouldn't a dark form have sprung out of the ground to hold a golden umbrella over him?

Well, that was that. From the personal angle, he summed up, a rich and rewarding experience. Professionally, a pure waste of time, except for the item that Madame Landini was telling people she had been persuaded to write her memoirs. The opinion poll showed Claudius and the Maharajah in conflict over the cause of Madame's breakdown; Claudius, who didn't know her but thought he knew the facts, thought that writing about her first husband hadn't upset her. The Maharajah—oldest friend, dearest friend, closest friend—held it to be the reason for her sudden halt. Perhaps the secretary down at Brighton could give a casting vote.

He set out after breakfast the next morning, irritated by the knowledge that although he had only fifty miles to cover, the first five would be a nose-to-tail procession making mileage meaningless. Sleet was beginning to fall, which would further delay his progress. He thought he might reach Brighton in time for a late lunch.

It was twelve-thirty when he arrived. He drove slowly along the familiar sea front— familiar because three years ago, when he came up from Cornwall to join the firm of D.S. Claud, he had made the experiment of living in rooms at Brighton and commuting; brought up on the very fringe of the Atlantic, he felt that he needed the sound and the smell of the sea. But commuting had proved a mistake; he had loathed the daily train journey, detested his fellow-commuters and the arrival at the noisy London terminus and the subsequent scramble on bus or Underground. After three months, he had moved to London.

He leaned forward at a traffic light, drew the paper with the secretary's address from the glove compartment of the car, and glanced at it. This girl, he thought, had a troublesome habit of settling herself in confusing districts: was this to be Yarrow Road or Street or Square?

It was none of these, he discovered. It was Yarrow Lane.

He drove along it, looking at the numbers. Baird, like Laird, he noted, had been forced to forego the elegant residential districts; this was a long way from the mansions and the sea. But perhaps she, too, had a view from a bathroom window? Number 6, 8, 10, 12—this was it.

He stopped and looked at it in perplexity; it was a shop. Outside it hung a sign: *Patisserie*. Through the sleet and the steam of the window, he could discern large trays filled with pastries of a kind he had not seen since he was on holiday in France. Hunger, sharp and saliva-producing, gripped him—why not go in and buy a dozen of those things and drive to the sea front and keep the car heater on and eat them, and to hell with waistline? This girl should be not Miss Baird but Miss Bun, the baker's daughter.

Then something made him glance once more at the paper on which the address was written. Not 12, but 12A. A pity, because 12 was that wonderful shop window, whereas 12A was an uninteresting door beyond it. This, he saw, was a street of shops, all of the same design, with living quarters on the floor above, but somebody had robbed a slice from Number 12 and built a separate entrance to the upper floor.

He got out of the car, shrugged hurriedly into his coat and turned up the collar, not before a gust of wind had blown an icy trickle down his neck. He walked to the door, pressed a bell and stood huddled, waiting for someone to answer the summons. After a pause which he thought far too long, he heard footsteps descending, and the door opened a little way. He saw a middle-aged woman with a face that still retained much of what must once have been considerable beauty. She had greying hair drawn neatly into a knot; she wore a white overall, its sleeves pushed up over shapely, floury forearms. When she spoke, it was in a friendly tone and with a slight foreign intonation.

'Please come in.' She opened the door wide and drew him inside. 'We cannot talk in the cold—and you will get wet.' She closed the door and faced him on the small square of carpet at the foot of a steep flight of stairs. 'Yes? What is it that you want?'

'May I see Miss Baird, please? She lives here, doesn't she?'

'She is out. I am her mother.' Was he imagining it, Rodney wondered, or had the friendly look given place to one of wariness? 'She did not say that anyone was coming to see her.'

'I've just driven down from London.'

'From London? To see her?'

'To talk to her about the job she was doing there. Will she be long?'

'Yes, very long.' There was no mistake about the withdrawal of cordiality; she was looking at him with a cold, hard stare. 'And to talk of the job,' she continued in a tone that matched the look, 'this is of no use. She has now got another position, so she will not be interested.

There is nothing more to be said. Goodbye.'

He opened his mouth to speak, but surprise and rage kept him silent. She had opened the door, seized his sleeve and swung him round to face the street; then she put a hand on his back, and if he had not braced himself, the force of the push she gave him would have sent him staggering on to the pavement. Behind him, the door banged. He turned with a vague idea of kicking it down, and then regained control of himself and got into the car and drove away. Come in, she had said, smiling. What had he said? Nothing. He had merely asked how long the girl would be out. It couldn't have been his appearance that upset her; if she hadn't liked the look of him, she wouldn't have invited him inside.

He found that he had stopped the car on the sea front and was sitting staring at the waves breaking on the shore. Snow had begun to fall. A fine day to choose, he thought bitterly, and all for nothing.

Well, not for nothing, he decided. He had an uncle living here; he would call on him. He was an anti-social old gentleman and he threw jugs of water over callers, but a kind of truce had been established three years ago, and this might be a good time to test it. He would fill in time by paying a call on his Uncle Julian, and then he would have beer and sandwiches at a pub, and after that he would drive back to Number 12A Yarrow Lane and hammer on the door until Miss Baird let him in, or he was given a good reason why he could not see her.

He drove to a wide street which in summer was tree-shaded. The few houses along each side of it were large, and each stood in spacious grounds. All but one had been converted to apartments or maisonettes; the exception was his uncle's, which remained unchanged, still handsome, still imposing—a house that had outlived its era.

He left the car at the gate, went in and used the heavy knocker on the front door—the bell, he knew, had long been disconnected. He waited, heard no sounds, and did not knock again; in or out, his uncle wasn't receiving, and this was no day to be doused with cold water.

He drove away, and at the end of the street turned in the direction of a well-remembered pub. The thought of food made him increase speed, and he did his best to beat the traffic light, stopping irritably as it turned to red. And what happened next he never, then or at any future time, tried to understand. You could only account for these things, he decided, if you dabbled in the occult. If, like himself, you merely believed in coincidence, you took what was offered and gave thanks. Especially when it was something as welcome and as wonderful as the picture reflected in his rear mirror.

Behind his car, a small van had drawn up. On its side was painted the word *Patisserie* in exact imitation of the sign above the shop door. It was driven by a girl wearing a scarlet-and-white woollen cap surmounted by a pompon. And one glance at the face below the cap, a younger edition of the face he had seen at Number 12A Yarrow Lane, left him in no doubt that he was looking at Nicola Baird.

CHAPTER THREE

There was no time to act; the traffic lights changed to green and Rodney was forced to move on. He drew his car to one side, let the van pass, and followed it. She knew her Brighton, he noted, driving in her wake in and out of side streets. Twice the van stopped, but before he could reach it, the girl had sounded the horn to alert a client, handed out a white-wrapped parcel, and driven on again. She drove fast, and snow was falling so fast that at times he feared he would lose her.

At last, in a wide street near the sea front, she stopped outside an apartment block. He brought his car alongside, got out and addressed her as she was taking a parcel from the back of the van.

'I'd like to talk to you, if you—'

She barely glanced at him. 'Busy,' she said, and banged the van door decisively.

He called after her rapidly-retreating back. 'Wait a minute, will you? My name's Laird,

Rodney Laird. I came down to see you.'

She had stopped and turned, and was looking at him with a frown.

'From D.S. Claud?'

'Yes. Where can we talk?'

'How did you know who I was?'

'Do I have to stand in a blizzard and explain?'

She gave the matter a moment's consideration.

'Wait in your car,' she instructed. 'I'll join you in a minute.'

He waited anxiously, peering out and wondering whether she would leap into the van and drive away, or perhaps turn inexplicably hostile, as her mother had done. But when she emerged from the building, she directed her steps towards the car. He got out and opened the door for her, experiencing as she neared him a feeling of surprise that Oliver had not mentioned her looks. But Oliver liked well-dressed women, and this one might not have qualified. If not smart, she was certainly picturesque, Rodney decided. She was wearing green woollen slacks with the ends tucked into short boots. Round her neck was a woollen scarf. Like himself, she wore an anorak, but hers had seen long and hard service.

She settled herself in the car beside him and put a calm question.

'Madame Landini wants to make friends?'

'No. I was sent down to talk to you, to try

67

and get a few more details about what happened.'

'Isn't she doing any talking?'

'No. She announced that she'd stopped writing her memoirs. Her doctor has ordered complete rest. What happened?'

'I gave Mr Armstrong all the details there were. How did you know who I was?'

'By your resemblance to your mother. I went to your house and—'

'—and she told you I was out making deliveries?'

'She told me nothing. She threw me out.'

'Is that a joke?'

'It's the truth. I went to Number 12A and she came to the door and asked me to step inside. One minute later, she threw or more accurately pushed me out. I drove away. I drew up at the traffic lights, and a van drew up behind me, and on it was the *Patisserie* sign, and driving it was a girl sufficiently like her mother to make me try to establish contact.'

'Pushed you out? I don't believe it, but if it's true, you must have said something, done something—'

'I rang the bell. She came downstairs. She saw how hard it was sleeting, so she smiled and very kindly drew me into shelter and closed the door. We stood at the foot of the stairs and I said I wanted to see you in connection with some work you'd been doing for us. Whereupon she opened the door again, got hold of my sleeve and when I was past her, put a hand in the middle of my back and shoved. Is that being thrown out?'

'Yes. Yes, that's being thrown out.' She had been frowning; now her face cleared. 'That must have made her feel a lot better.'

'I don't understand.'

'She was just letting off steam.'

'Oh, is that all? I'm sorry she picked me to—'

'She's the gentlest, kindest, nicest person you could meet.'

'When she's not shoving strangers into the sleet.'

'Something upset her.'

'Not me.'

'Not directly—but you're part of it. You . . . Look, I've got to do the rest of these deliveries. Could we meet somewhere?'

'No. I'd like to keep my eye on you. I'll follow the van.'

'Don't be silly. Just name a place, and I'll be there. Have you had lunch?'

'No. I was going to have beer and sandwiches in a pub, and after that, I'd made up my mind to make another assault on Number 12A. If you don't like eating in pubs, I could—'

'I'm given a free lunch at the *patisserie*.'

'Tell them you've had another free offer. I'll wait for you outside the shop.'

It was not a long wait. He saw the van come into sight, pass him and go round the corner.

Following, he saw Nicola backing it into a garage. Then she went into the shop to inform them that she would be lunching out.

They said little on the way to the pub. Rodney had to concentrate on driving; snow was now falling so thickly that it was settling on the windscreen, and the roads were dangerously slippery. It was with relief that they entered the warm, comfortable lounge and made unhesitatingly for the leather-covered armchairs near the fire.

'Did you ever hear that old song about "London by the sea, that's the place for me"?' he asked, as he hung up their coats.

'No. Sing it.'

'Some other time. It was once the place for me—for over two months.'

'You lived here, in Brighton?'

'Yes. My first experience of commuting, and I hope my last. The same faces, the same platform, the same papers under the same arms, the same remarks about the weather, the same—'

'I've got it: you disliked commuting. Are you as hungry as I am?'

'They've got ham and cheese and slices off a joint. Do you want it here by the fire, or up at the counter?'

'Oh, here. Beef with lots of mustard, please, and maybe tongue too. You can order cakes, if you want them; they buy them from the *patisserie*.'

'No cakes. Beer?'

'Failing hot punch, yes.'

He carried the food and the glasses and bottles to a table beside them. After the first sandwich, she pulled off her cap and shook her hair free, and it fell to her shoulders, straight and soft and silky, in colour what he termed browny-blonde. Her manner was easy, her speech casual to the point of flippancy. Her glance was direct and—when a gleam of sardonic humour shone in her eyes—disconcerting.

'When you can talk, talk,' he said.

'About Madame? Well, it was short and sharp. And a shock, because I'd begun to think she rather liked me. We'd certainly got on well over the work, and during the last week I'd even been promoted to lunching with her—which I'd rather not have done, because there was much too much of everything and I kept remembering the hungry poor. Besides that, when my food was sent into my office room, I could get a break. The last day, I took the last sheets I'd typed into her sitting room, where she spent most of her day. She read them through and then told me I could go home, and said she was sorry she'd kept me late. Then she got up and patted my cheek and said I mustn't allow her to overwork me. I would have liked to tell her that so long as I got overtime pay, I wouldn't mind the overtime, but all I did was thank her and say good night. When I got to

71

the door, she said I was to be sure and make a note of all the extra hours—and that's how we parted. I went into the room farther along the corridor, a room I kept my things in, got into my storm suit and came out—and she was waiting at the head of the stairs, just standing—'

'Did you work in that room?'

'No. I worked on the ground floor. The room was only for my personal use during the day. When I came out, she was there, staring. Not staring, glaring. She had the sheets I'd given her in her hand, and suddenly she tore at them—really tore them to pieces—and hurled them at me. Most of the pieces went over the banisters. She was a kind of yellow colour, and her eyes looked like an animal's. I couldn't believe she was the gracious, queenly creature I'd seen a few minutes before. I remember thinking that when I got to be an old woman, I'd never let the veils drop, as she'd done; there was something horrible about her, ugly and terribly pathetic, I couldn't have spoken if I'd tried, but if I had spoken, she wouldn't have heard, because she'd begun to shout. Servants came running from all directions, but she didn't seem to see them; she was too intent on yelling at me.'

'What did she actually say?'

'Nothing very coherent or connected. As far as I remember, she said I was to remove myself from her sight and never let me see her again. I thought she must suddenly have gone out of her mind—she must have, mustn't she? I went down the stairs, and for once nobody preceded me to clear a passage or followed me to hold up my train. I had to let myself out. And that's all.'

'Not quite. Do you think it was the strain or the pain of writing about the past that—'

'What pain or strain, for heaven's sake? Pain or strain? I took most of it down from dictation while she reclined on a sofa in her sitting room, stopping now and then to take a phone call, or make one, or receive a guest, or order tea or coffee or hot chocolate for us both, or send for her manicurist or her masseuse or her hairdresser or chiropodist, or her chauffeur to give orders, or her chef to discuss the next banquet. The next person to write a book will be myself, all about high life. She tossed off details of her past just like someone reading items out of an old engagement book.'

'But the tragedy of her first husband's death—'

'I told you there was no pain or strain, and there wasn't. The details of what you've just called a tragedy—which it was—were dictated in between negotiations for the sale of the Landini palace, sorry *palazzo*, which she's selling to a Maharajah. Before I went to work for her, I thought that the expression about somebody being so rich that they didn't know what they were worth, was a ... a figure of speech. It isn't. Madame Landini doesn't

73

know. All her millions are looked after by this Italian who's called Signor Piozzi, who also looks after the Maharajah's millions. She doesn't have to give them a thought. Anything that involves money is taken care of for her; she says to this Signor Piozzi: "Guido, you will arrange this?"—and he does. I don't think I could have taken it much longer. I've got a piggy-bank mind and I'm stuck with the idea that if you want money, you have to earn it. Another month with Madame, and I'd have become a Marcher. So for the last time, no pain and no strain.'

'Don't you think it could have been a financial crisis of some kind?'

'No.'

'That attitude of not interesting herself in financial details could be a pose.'

'It could be, in anybody else. In her, no. She doesn't think about money in the way that she doesn't think about driving her car; she leaves driving to the chauffeur and finance to Signor Piozzi and sits back and let them do what they're being paid to do. The only time—before the outburst—that I ever saw her stirred out of her sleep was when she was dictating the part about where her first husband took the flowers off the deck and down to their suite, and forgot to come back—but I didn't think she was feeling grief, I thought she was just angry because Fate, for once, had treated her just like anybody else.'

'Claudius said much the same thing. He was on board.'

'On board the *Atlantis*?'

'Not travelling. Seeing somebody off.'

'You mean he was there when it happened?'

'He was there just before it happened. Anton Veitch passed quite close to him as he was carrying the flowers off the deck. Later, the people Claudius had been seeing off wrote from New York to describe what had happened, and their opinion was that the Princess's reaction wasn't so much grief as fury.'

'That checks. So if you want to find a reason for her giving up the memoirs, don't imagine it was the pain of recalling her first husband, poor fellow.'

'Poor?'

'Of course, poor. Do you wonder he took a dive overboard? How would you have liked to be in his shoes, dragging round the world as her accompanist? He should have been giving concerts of his own—he was a sensational pianist. Didn't you read what she wrote?'

'Yes, but—'

'But what? He fell in love with her, or she made him think he was in love, and they got married, and that was the end of his career.'

'He might have decided that as her husband and her accompanist, he'd get as far as he would have done on his own as a concert pianist. He—'

75

Her sound of contempt halted him.

'Did you say you'd read what she'd written?' she demanded.

'Yes. And that's my opinion. What's yours?'

'That you must be pretty insensitive. Have you ever met a pianist, a right-at-the-top, brilliant-future concert pianist?'

'No.'

'Neither have I. But I know that after all those years of work, and early success, with the audiences standing up to give him an oration, he—'

'Ovation.'

'—he couldn't have enjoyed trailing on to platforms in the wake of his wife and sitting down with a piece of music in front of him marked: Vamp Till Ready.'

'There's no evidence to suggest that he ever—'

'He ended up in the English Channel, didn't he? Don't you call that evidence?'

'Have it your own way. What upset your mother?'

'I did. I hadn't been home for some time. When I took the job with Madame Landini, my mother was in Switzerland. She got back yesterday and so did I—with the news that I'd been sacked. What upset her, I think, wasn't the fact that I'd been sacked, but the manner of the sacking. She always gets a bit excited when I come home. This time, she bustled round and said she'd get tea ready, and while she was bustling, I went into my room and began to unpack. The rooms we live in, above the shop, aren't exactly large. I left my bedroom door open, and we could talk without my having to raise my voice. I told her where I'd been working, and made what I thought was a very funny story of how I'd been evicted and . . . Do I mean evicted, or would you like to make that ejected?'

'Yes. Go on.'

'I realised, after a little while, that the story couldn't have been as amusing as I'd thought. She wasn't laughing, and when I came to think of it, she'd stopped bustling. I looked into the living room and saw her sitting on a chair staring straight in front of her, with her face as white as a sheet and tears pouring—really pouring down her cheeks. I mopped them up, but I saw I'd really shaken her. I myself didn't in the least mind being yelled at by Madame Landini because I felt so sorry for her, looking the way she did—but my mother obviously took the view that I'd been insulted, not to say humiliated. So now you can see what a pleasure it must have been to get some of her own back on somebody who was connected with the Landini. Do they give you coffee here?'

'Yes, but I wouldn't really recommend it.'

'Then let's go home. My mother makes wonderful coffee—Swiss-style.'

'In a moment. I want to clear up one or two

77

points.'

'Point one?'

'If Madame Landini recovered from whatever it is she's suffering from, and decided to go on with her memoirs, would you agree to going back to work for her?'

'She said she never wanted to see me again.'

'That was part of the breakdown. I think when she recovers, she'll want you to go back. Would you go?'

Something in his tone made her pause before replying. She studied him for some moments and then put a question in her turn.

'How much would you care if she never finished her memoirs?'

He frowned.

'We'd look fools, of course; people would say we rushed her into it too fast, or made a mess of it. I'd be sorry on D.S. Claud's account; it's the only big thing he's ever had a chance to bring out, and as he can't go on much longer, it would have made a nice happy ending for him. Perhaps one of the reasons Madame Landini has halted is because she's decided that his imprint doesn't carry enough prestige—but if I know her, she checked that before letting him have the book.'

'She told me it was through you.'

'So it was, in a way, and I was glad because it was a chance to pay back something to Claudius.'

'You owed him something?'

'He published a book of mine.'

'You write books?'

'Not any more. Just that one. No more.'

'Why not?'

'No gift, no talent, not even any desire to write any more. Besides discovering that I couldn't write, I discovered that it's a lonely profession. I wanted to move in a world of writers, not to shut myself up with one book. And I wanted to move in a book world, not to bury myself in a remote corner of Cornwall.'

'I've heard of people writing books in London. Why did it have to be Cornwall?'

'That's where my home is. I hadn't long been down from Oxford, and I announced that I'd decided to become a writer. My father thought—said—that I was off my head, but my mother persuaded him to let me live in the gardener's cottage while I produced my masterpiece. The book might have gone better if she hadn't come down every hour or so to ask whether I was cold or hot or hungry or thirsty or comfortable—or if my sister hadn't brought her friends down to peer through the windows to watch an author at work.'

'What was the book about?'

'War. A re-hash of Napoleon's campaigns, with Bonaparte on the move, while from up above, Alexander the Great and Julius Caesar looked down and watched what he was doing, and told each other how he should have done it. I'd read history at Oxford and thought the idea was magnificent, but the book never got off the battleground. My father, who's ex-Royal Navy, took to looking in and trying to persuade me to switch from generals to admirals, so that he could give me a few tips. After a time, all I wanted to do was throw the damned thing into the sea, but I had to justify all those impressive speeches I'd made before moving into the gardener's cottage. So I finished the book, and it was refused by fifteen publishers—and then D.S. Claud wrote to say they'd take it. Nobody'll ever know how I felt when I read that letter. It put a brand on me—D.S. Claud's.'

'Did the book sell?'

'Are you crazy? It fell dead on the printing press. The thing is that Claudius took it. I'm not only grateful for myself; my mother still goes round telling her friends what a pity it was I gave up a successful writing career to go into publishing. Even my father can be heard muttering that I gave it up against his wishes. So there's the answer—rather a long answer—to your question as to whether I care whether Madame Landini goes on, or doesn't go on. If she does, will you?'

'I might. Do you think she'll finish the book?'

He hesitated.

'It doesn't seem to me,' he said at last, 'that her outburst was connected with the book. You said she read through the last sheets you'd typed, and passed them. What I think is that during the time you were putting on what you called your storm suit, she had a telephone call that upset her—a call from whom, or what about, we're not likely to find out.'

'I thought of that. It was the only reason I could find for what she did. I wondered if the Maharajah had rung up to say he wasn't coming, after all. That would have shaken her; she'd made some expensive preparations for his reception.'

'He came. I saw him when I went to the house yesterday.'

'Then that kills my only theory. Was he wearing a diamond-studded suit?'

'No. He was in Indian dress.'

'Perhaps he'll calm her down and make her start writing again. If she doesn't, then what?'

'We'll be no worse off than we were before. Shall we go and get this coffee?'

He paid the bill and they went out to the car, making a dash through the snow and shivering until the car heater began its work.

'Did you say your mother was Swiss?' he asked.

'I said her coffee was. She's Swiss-born, the daughter of a Swiss pastrycook who worked in England and got himself naturalised—her, too—but decided in the end to go back to Switzerland. My mother stayed in England and got married, and she and my father—he was English—started the shop; his main job was keeping the accounts and ordering stores and sending out bills. When he died, my mother found she couldn't run the place alone, so my grandfather came over from Switzerland to help—but he was too old to do it for long, and the business began to run down. If I'd been older, I could have helped, but I was five when my father died and twelve when my grandfather died, so I wasn't much use. When I was sixteen, I decided to leave school and take a hand. I used what money there was to divide the house into top and bottom, and we let off the shop and the rooms behind it, and live upstairs. That way, we get the rent and we also get jobs helping with the making and distribution of the pastries. That's my life history up to date.'

'Not quite. When did you start working in London?'

'Two years ago, when I was twenty-one. It was my mother's idea. She thought that once I got out of *patisserie* circles and up to London, I'd fall in with the rich and the great—and you see how right she was. Before the Landini job, I didn't do too well. I'm not highly qualified, and the money I earned didn't go very far. If my mother had ever seen the dump I lived in, she would have died right on its dirty doorstep—but I kept her away.'

'How many people do you know in London?'

'People—or men? If you mean men, I don't

82

have to stay home if I feel like going out. I never had a job that came within miles of the Landini one, as far as interest goes. I can see why you want to bring the book out. I've never typed memoirs before, but they can't all be like hers. The only thing...'

'Well?'

'She juggles with the truth now and again. I mean, when she's talking. For instance, that story she tells everyone, about how you saved her from being eaten by a dog—it's never the same twice. So how true are the memoirs?'

'That's what Claudius was wondering. Oliver doesn't think it matters; he says if people ever get a chance to read the memoirs, they'll be too deeply interested to stop and ponder about inaccuracies.'

'Oliver? Oh, that's Oliver Tallent. Straight out of Madame Tussaud's.'

'Rubbish. Oliver's all right.'

'That's just what he said about you, when I remarked that I didn't think you should have taken off for America for a whole month, leaving Madame Landini without her park patrolman. He said in that warm, excitable, enthusiastic manner of his that you were doing wonders over there, promoting the book. Why does he change his women so frequently? I had to go to his house twice, with typescript, and each time there was a different woman in residence. What attracts them?'

'He does.'

'Not for long, apparently.'

'No girl has ever left him. He—'

'—throws them out, the way my mother threw you?'

'He's a bad judge of women, that's all. He always hopes that a girl he likes will—'

'—stick, but she doesn't?'

'Will you allow me to—'

'present his softer side? Go ahead.'

'He wants to find a wife and settle down, but the type he chooses doesn't seem interested in settling down. None of his girl friends has any nest-building qualities.'

'Not qualities. Instincts.'

'Instincts. So that's what keeps happening—he starts something, and the thing folds.'

'How did two men as different as you and O. Tallent ever get to be friends?'

'Our families live within a mile of each other in Cornwall. We went to the same schools and we were up at Oxford together. Then he became a literary agent and asked me to join him, but when I came to London to see D.S. Claud, he offered me a job in his firm.'

'And, still warm with gratitude, you took it?'

'You might put it that way.'

'How else would ... You can't go down that street—it's one-way.'

'I wasn't going to go down it. I just stopped to look at it. I've got an uncle living in that house—Victoria Lodge.'

84

She turned to look at him in surprise.

'That's Sir Julian Mull's house—is he your uncle?'

'Yes.'

'You shouldn't tell people. They might think it ran in the family.'

'You think he's crazy?'

'Would you rather I called him eccentric?'

'Much rather. Did you go to his house and get water thrown at you?'

'No, but I know people who did. I've seen him around. He does his shopping in our district. Everybody knows who he is, and if you think it isn't crazy for a man of his age to go out in weather like this, for instance, without even a coat, and if you think it's merely eccentric to empty jugs of water on to harmless people who knock on his door—'

'He only gets annoyed if they go on knocking. He's not deaf; if he wanted to answer the door, then he would, wouldn't he? If he doesn't, why should he let people go on hammering and battering?'

'Why does he stay in that great house all by himself?'

'He can't afford servants.'

'Afford! Just think what the house must be worth! He could sell it and live in comfort in some nice, small—'

'He sold it years ago. The family lawyers bought it and they let him live in it rent free. He couldn't move to a smaller house. He needs large rooms.'

'What for?'

'Would you like to go and see?'

'What about that coffee?'

'It'll keep. As a matter of fact, I'd rather like a word with him, if he lets us in and I can talk to him. He was out in India all his working life, in the Indian Civil Service, and he might be able to tell me where I heard the name Hardanipur.'

'He's Madame Landini's Maharajah.'

'Yes, he is. When she first mentioned his name, I had an idea I'd heard it before, but I couldn't think where. If I heard my uncle mention it, it must have been in my extreme youth, because he and my father quarrelled when I was about four or five, and he hasn't been down to Cornwall since then. And I hadn't set eyes on him until I came to live at Brighton and looked him up.'

'Did he throw water on you?'

'Yes, the first time. After that, I got clever at dodging.'

He started the car and turned down the next street and then at the end of it turned again to approach his uncle's house.

'Why hasn't he got any money?' Nicola asked, as he stopped the car at the gate.

'He lost it. He thought up a scheme to double his capital, and the scheme backfired, and then he wrote to my mother to tell her he'd discovered the flaw in his scheme, and could now make her rich and get his own money back too. My father was at sea; by the time he'd got her letter telling him she'd handed over her money, it was too late to do anything. My father never forgave him.'

'Did your mother?'

'Yes. Her only complaint was that he sold all the furniture that was in this house without giving her a chance to buy any of it. She and my uncle were both born and brought up in the house, and she would have liked to see some of the stuff in our house in Cornwall. She's a bit vague in some ways; I don't think she ever realised quite how much money he'd poured down the drain—but my father knew. He and my uncle had a row which stopped just short of a shooting match, and after that, Uncle Julian passed out of our lives. My mother hasn't seen him since the row. When I was living here, she came up and paid me a visit and tried to see him, but he wouldn't let her in until she brought a written retraction from my father of all the harsh things he'd said. She was sorry not to get another look at the inside of the house.'

'What's she like?'

'Far from social, but not anti-social like Uncle Julian. She gets busy on odd things like pollination experiments and cross-breeding. At the moment she's keeping Chinese geese.'

He got out and opened the gate and then drove the car to the front door. Before he could knock, a window on the ground floor opened and a head was thrust out.

87

'What the devil d'you mean by driving in? Clear out, d'you hear?'

'I've brought a beautiful girl to see you.'

'Then take her away.'

Nicola had left the car and was standing beside Rodney, studying with frank interest the thin, lined, angry face at the window.

'What are you staring at?' Sir Julian asked irritably. 'I suppose you think I'm off my head?'

'Rodney said you weren't. How about proving it, one way or the other?'

'Eh?'

'I said—'

'Come round the back,' Sir Julian ordered.

He unlocked the back door to admit them. He was wearing a pair of shapeless corduroy trousers and a warm sweater. From the front, he looked totally bald; when he turned, his stringy grey hair could be seen springing from the top of his head and straggling down to his collar.

He led them into a room which, once a commodious kitchen, had been turned into a living room. A small electric fire stood on the outdated range; in spite of this, the room temperature was lower than that in Rodney's rooms in London. Near the fire was a low, cushioned cane chair. The dresser, bare of plates, now held rows of heavy books. On the table lay the remains of a meal: bread, cheese, yoghurt, sliced onions, unsliced tomatoes and a jug of coffee.

'Instant,' Nicola said, bending over to smell it. 'If you had any coffee beans, I could show you—'

'I have no coffee beans and I do not require to be shown anything, and I'd rather you didn't touch those books.'

She had taken down a large volume.

'*Religions of the World*,' she read, and opened it. 'Look, gods. Hindu gods.'

'Wrong,' snapped Sir Julian. 'You're looking at Lakshmi, the goddess—not the god—of prosperity.'

'Did you ever see a nicer hat?' Nicola turned a page. 'And look, another heavenly hat. Oh, and look at this one—two heads and two lovely hats.'

Sir Julian took the volume from her and replaced it with its fellows.

'She can't get her mind off hats,' he growled. 'Rodney, take her away.'

'Certainly. But while we're on India, I have a question.'

'Well, out with it.'

'Would it have been from you that I heard, in the distant past, the name Hardanipur?'

His uncle stared at him for a few seconds in the utmost amazement. Then he spoke angrily.

'No. Certainly not. Absolutely not. I am quite certain I never mentioned the name in your hearing, or in your parents' either.'

'You wouldn't by any chance know the

Maharajah of Hardanipur?'

'What d'you want to know for?'

'Just curiosity. He's connected with one of our authors. You knew him?'

It was clear that Sir Julian was debating whether to pursue the subject, or close it. He spoke reluctantly.

'I knew him probably better than any other Englishman did. I was Resident at Hardanipur for a time.'

'Resident?' Nicola repeated inquiringly.

'Don't you know what a Resident was?'

'No. I'm not even sure what a Maharajah is.'

'Then you're not very well-informed. A Maharajah means great prince or great ruler. I suppose you understand that I'm talking of the days when the British ruled India?'

'Now that you've told me, I do. So what's a Resident?'

'He was a member of the Political Department of the Indian Civil Service who was sometimes appointed by the British to live in a native State and keep an eye on political and financial matters. If you're going to think of the Maharajahs of those days, you've got to think of them in terms of royalty. They were chiefs who had pretty well complete control of all that went on within their boundaries, and when I speak of boundaries, you can think of some States as half the size of Wales. The Maharajahs held court, and they held durbars from time to time, to entertain visiting

90

potentates or, it may be, the Viceroy. Their private spending was their own affair, unless it outran the bounds of reason—but they had to keep their hands off the State revenue and the State regalia and the State jewels. Are you following me?'

'Yes.'

'The Maharajah of Hardanipur was one of the most important princes. He was entitled to a salute of fifteen guns. This was reduced, in my time, to ten.'

'Why?' Rodney asked.

'Long story, and none of your business. And it's all dead and gone.'

'If it's all dead and gone, then how does this Maharajah come to have so many millions?' Nicola asked.

'By being more far-seeing than his fellow-princes. He was clever enough, cunning enough, if you like, to make an early switch from native prince to merchant prince. He made his own estimate of what was going to happen when the British left, and he began to build his own empire. Today, he and his sons are joint owners of an industrial kingdom, and because it's a family concern, it's got a unity and cohesion and togetherness that no joint stock company ever managed to attain. It had a good start, of course—some twenty millions which he'd managed to get out of Hardanipur.'

'A crook?' Rodney asked.

'It depends who's talking. In my view, he's a

splendid chap. But if you ever come across him, I'd rather you didn't mention my name. Is that understood?'

'Yes.'

'Good. Now don't let me keep you.'

'There's one thing more. Couldn't you show Nicola—'

'No. Didn't I tell you from the start that I wouldn't have you bringing a string of your friends down here and expecting me to let them loose round the place?'

'Have I ever brought anybody before?'

'No.'

'Then treat this as a special case.'

Sir Julian hesitated. Then he turned and went abruptly out of the room, motioning to them to follow. He went through a large, empty, marble-floored hall, stopped at a door on the far side, waited for the others to catch up with him, and then unlocked it.

There were three long rooms opening into one another. All the windows along one side reached to the floor, and all overlooked the sea—but nobody entering could have looked at the view. There was no furniture, and all the doors had been removed. On the parquet floor, stretching through the three rooms and curving out of sight into other rooms unseen, were railway lines. They ran straight, they curved, they went over hills and into valleys, disappeared into tunnels and came out again, branching, crossing, recrossing. In sidings stood a dozen trains, freight or passenger, their engines gleaming, varying in type from early locomotives to the latest streamlined models. All were over two feet in length. A small kitten could have travelled comfortably in one of the freight cars. There were stations and signals, mail vans and cattle trucks and sleeping cars. The only floor space not covered with lines or stations were the spaced oblongs designed to allow Sir Julian to step without displacing the track.

Nicola, speechless, stood and stared. Then she turned to Sir Julian, to find that he had forgotten her. He had stepped to a wall on which was a large, complicated switchboard topped by a clock. He was checking the time by his own watch.

'Got to send off the Bombay Mail,' he muttered.

He pulled a lever. The Bombay Mail moved slowly, gathered speed and travelled unerringly along its complicated route. The pace was even, the curves rounded with steadiness and safety.

'Madras Mail's late. Been trouble down there,' he said. 'Line damaged for a time.'

The Madras Mail set off, its driver clearly determined to make up time. It raced through tunnels and outstripped the Delhi Express, which had been sent on its journey. The Darjeeling Mail moved out of its siding, took a wide circle round the room, went through a doorway and began to climb a realistic mountain built on one side of a staircase. Reaching the top, it moved along one of the stairs to the mountain on the other side, and began its descent. The Mount Everest Funicular went straight up the track built on the stairs, and stopped at Camp Two.

'That's as far as I've taken it,' Sir Julian explained. 'I wanted to finish a new route I've got running across the Sind Desert. Time you went,' he proceeded without pause. 'Shut all the doors as you go and don't go chattering about this to your friends. I won't be treated like a zoo.'

They left him adjusting his timetables.

'Well, crazy or eccentric?' Rodney asked as they drove away.

'I can see where all the money went. Those engines...'

'Yes. Expensive. He has them specially made up in Darlington.'

'How did you get in in the first place?'

'I climbed in through a back window. I'd gone to see him two or three times; the third time, there was dead silence, so I got in to see if he was all right. He was. Then one day I saw him out walking on the sea front. He'd stopped and was gazing out to sea and it occurred to me that there he was, able to see miles of sea from his house, and perhaps it would give him an interest to watch the shipping. So I drove to my room, fetched my telescope and rigged it up in

94

one of his upper windows. He never mentioned it, and neither did I; I don't know whether he uses it or not. I thought I was giving him a nice hobby; I had not the slightest idea he studied world religions or owned a railway system.'

He stopped the car at the door of Number 12A and stood beside Nicola as she got out her latchkey.

'I think I'd better say goodbye,' he said. 'If you give me your phone number, I'll be able to get hold of you if anything develops.'

'We came here for coffee. Are you frightened of my mother?'

'I don't want to pull the switch again. Incidentally, if Madame Landini decides to continue, can you get out of this job you've fixed up?'

She opened the door.

'Deliveries? That's not a job. I just help out whenever I'm home.'

'Your mother said you had another job.'

She stopped to stare at him, but he thought it too cold to pursue the topic on the doorstep. He repeated the statement when he was following her up the steep stairway.

'She said you'd taken another job.'

'That was to make sure you didn't come back.' She raised her voice and called, but there was no reply. 'She's out, but I make coffee almost as well as she does. We usually talk French or German; which do you prefer?'

'English. I always feel—'

95

He stopped abruptly. He had reached the top of the stairs and was looking round the living room. She turned to take his coat and saw on his face an expression she was unable to identify.

'What's the matter?' she asked.

He did not answer. To speak would have meant trying to explain that here, at last, was his dream of the perfect home: simple, within his means, spotless, comfortable ... homelike. His eyes took in the plain wooden floor, mirror-bright, the low chairs, the neat bookshelves, the fresh flowers by the window, the snowy curtains.

'I like this house,' he said inadequately at last.

'It's only half a house. I used to be sorry we couldn't see the sea—it seemed silly to be living on the coast and see nothing but houses all round. But you can hear the sea. Not often; at night, and sometimes during the day when there's a minute or two without traffic noises. In the silence, you can hear the sea.' She opened a door. 'Come into the kitchen and sit down while I get things ready.'

He sat on a wooden chair, on the seat of which was tied a blue cushion. He watched coffee being taken from a jar and ground in an electric mill. When she opened cupboards, he saw neat rows of stores or crockery; in the refrigerator stood lines of plastic containers. This was a home, he thought, a place poised between the extremes of his father's battleship order and the mess that Angela called a lived-in look.

He carried the tray into the living room. As he set it down on the table, he heard the sound of a latchkey. Nicola came in holding a third cup, and called down the stairs.

'Hot coffee to warm you up,' she said. 'And a visitor.' She waited for her mother to reach the top. 'Rodney Laird.'

Mrs Baird was wearing a small fur hat and a coat of the same shade as Nicola's anorak. Her cheeks were reddened by the cold, taking years off her age and making her resemblance to Nicola even more striking. Rodney thought that in her youth, she must have been even lovelier than her daughter.

Her manner was composed, but scarcely friendly.

'You are welcome, Mr Laird.'

'Then why did you throw him out?' Nicola asked.

'I did not throw him out. Don't be absurd, Nicola; you're talking nonsense.'

'He said you did. Give me your coat. Coffee?'

'No, thank you. I have just had some, downstairs. They told me you didn't have lunch today.'

'They're wrong. I did—with Rodney. I spent the time trying to erase the bad impression you'd made.'

'Don't be silly. I hope you don't take her seriously, Mr Laird. She jokes about everything, even about things that are not for joking.'

'Even about love,' Nicola said dreamily. 'When I was twelve, I wrote a poem for the school magazine. Want to hear it?'

'It was simply rubbish,' Mrs Baird told him.

'First verse coming up,' Nicola said. 'So far as I can remember, it went: *Love is a beverage offered to me, Shall I accept it? I'll sip it, and see.* How's that for budding talent? Unfortunately, the bud didn't open.'

'Did you say you were twelve?' Rodney asked.

'Thereabouts. Verse two: *Love is a shrouded form beckoning to me, Shall I approach it? I'll unveil it—and see.* Not as good as verse one. It didn't get into the magazine.'

'Rejected on the grounds of undue precocity?'

'No. I was told it didn't scan.'

'If you have finished talking nonsense,' her mother said, 'you could pass me Mr Laird's empty cup. If I didn't welcome you when you came before, Mr Laird, it was because I lost my head a little. I thought you wished to speak of Madame Landini, and I didn't want to hear anything about her. I will never forgive her for the way she behaved to Nicola.'

'I came down,' Rodney explained, 'to try and get a clearer picture of what happened, and

98

to find out what led up to Madame's outburst.'

'And have you discovered?'

'No. Except that it wasn't, as far as one can judge, connected with the memoirs. If she decides to go on with them—'

'No,' broke in Mrs Baird. Her tone was almost passionate. 'This, no. If you are going to say that you wish Nicola to go back to work for her, then to this I will absolutely not agree. I cannot prevent her, but I have said what I wish: that she will not go.'

'Listen, Mother. I—'

'No, Nicola, I won't listen. Some other girl could do the work just as well as you—what is it, after all? Only typing. It can be done by any other girl. I don't like to interfere or put myself in your way, but I ask you not to go back.'

There was silence. Nicola, seated on the floor beside an electric radiator, finished her coffee, handed the cup to Rodney and then spoke slowly.

'I'm almost certain,' she said, 'that Madame Landini won't go on with her memoirs. If she doesn't, I'll be sorry because I think the book ought to be written. I don't like her, but every time I've settled down to type what she'd drafted or dictated, I've forgotten where I was. I was ... Rodney, could I use the word transported?'

'If it fits.'

'Isn't it what they used to do to criminals in the old days?'

'Yes. You were saying?'

'That I was transported when I typed the memoirs. I was carried away. I thought, when I first took the job, that I'd just be typing out a list of triumphs and famous names, with Madame Landini in the centre of the stage and the rest seen dimly in the background—but it didn't turn out to be like that. It's exciting. It's fascinating. Nothing small ever seemed to happen to her. Wherever history was happening, there she was, ever since she was born. At the end of every day, I looked forward to starting on the next stage. If there's to be any more, I'd like to go back and be there to the end. And there's another angle. I haven't seen much of poor old Mr Claud, but I know the book means a lot to the firm. If Madame Landini goes back to work, and if she decides she'd like me to go back to work too, then I will.'

'Very well. I can't stop you,' Mrs Baird said. 'But after she acted as she did, you are wrong to go back.'

Rodney was preparing to leave. Nicola went to a desk, wrote something on a piece of paper and brought it to him.

'Telephone number,' she said. 'Thank you for the lunch.'

He shook Mrs Baird's hand.

'Goodbye. I hope you won't be angry if Nicola goes back—but if she does, I promise to keep an eye on her.'

'Thank you.' The hand in his was cold. He

100

went down the stairs with Nicola, and drove away.

He had hoped to get back to London in time to look into the office, but at seven he was still on the outskirts. He stopped and telephoned to Oliver.

'Just back,' he told him.

'Come and have dinner. I'll order something hot.'

'Are you alone?'

'Until ten-thirty.'

'Good. Heat some rum for me, will you?'

He found the front door on the latch, and Oliver in his bath. He helped himself to hot rum-and-orange and stretched out on the deep-cushioned sofa.

'Any news?' he called.

'None this end. How about you?'

'Nothing. The only thing is that Nicola Baird will come back if we need her.'

'If she doesn't get tired of waiting, and get another job. Pour me out some of that stuff, will you?'

Rodney took the drink, with his own, into the bedroom and lowered himself carefully on to the bed, which was of cushioned suede set almost at ground level.

'Her mother,' he said, 'is dead against her coming back. It's a Swiss background—pastrycooks.' He put his glass on the floor, and stretched. 'My God, it was cold down there. Resorts are pretty dreary in the winter, too. I can't believe I stuck more than two months of it. What are we going to eat?'

'Soup and steak. And there it comes. Open the door, will you? Don't pay; just tip the man. And lay a table.'

Rodney found a cloth, spread it on a table and laid out the food. Oliver, coming in in the Japanese robe, began to lift everything off again. He folded the cloth, fetched another from a drawer and spread it on the central table.

'Wrong cloth, wrong table,' he explained.

'Henrietta's turning you into a handy little housekeeper. Do I use this napkin, or do I have to wait while you fetch the right one?'

'Don't carp. Eat.'

Rodney ate, but something in the air—the spirit of Henrietta, he thought—had made him lose his desire to talk over the events of the day, to give Oliver a sketch of the Baird background and in doing so clarify some of the half-formed impressions in his own mind. He helped to put the empty plates and dishes back into the container that was to be returned to the restaurant, and then decided to leave.

He got home just before half past ten. Walking from the garage to the house, he was confronted by Mrs Major's dustbin, which had been carried to the Grelbys' doorstep, and left there. He picked it up and heard Peter Grelby speaking behind him.

'It's no use, you know. I've taken it back

102

twice, and she's dumped it here again.'

Rodney turned. 'It might be easier to put it on wheels,' he suggested.

'Not a bad idea. I've been hoping I'd run into you, to thank you for letting us use your phone. And also to ask you if you can do anything to stop that old harridan from making a ruddy nuisance of herself.'

'I try, now and then.'

'She's been a blasted pain ever since we moved in. Why has she got it in for us? You'd think she'd be pleased to see this street being smartened up.'

'She's not pleased.'

'I know that. Priss went to see her when we first came, to ask whether she'd come and clean the house once or twice a week. The answer, a very rude one, was no. She worked for you, didn't she?'

'Until Angela came. Now she only comes up now and again to clean up the worst messes.'

'Then she's got plenty of free hours, which is what Priss pointed out.'

'A great mistake, pointing it out.'

'I know. All she got was abuse. I'm certain the old witch bribes all those wild kids who come stampeding round here sometimes. Can't you tell her she's overdoing it? What's her basic complaint?'

'The loss of all her old friends and neighbours.'

'Then why doesn't she follow them? Most of

them have moved into those new apartment blocks, haven't they? Why doesn't she go and join them?'

Rodney thought it would be tactless to explain that she found it more stimulating to stay where she was. He picked up the dustbin and went as far as to guarantee that it would not be moved again—at least, not that night. He placed it in front of Mrs Major's doorstep, and found her waiting for him in the hall.

'Now, wot did you go an' do that for?' she demanded.

'You're a spiteful old woman,' he told her without heat, 'and one of these days, I'm going to stop supplying you with free bottles of my home-made wine. Furthermore, someone's soon going to report you to the police for disturbing the peace of the neighbourhood. You'll do somebody some real damage if you go on leaving that dustbin in the middle of the pavement on a dark night like this.'

'D'you know what she come and said to me, that little snippet? "I need a cleanin' woman," she said. Those were 'er first words, just like that.'

'She didn't want to waste your time, so she came straight to the point.'

'I went straight to the point, too, an' told 'er she wasn't gettin' none o' me time.'

'She needs help in the house.'

'She's young, ain't she? At 'er age, I could've gorn over three 'ouses that size, all in one

104

mornin'. She's lazy, that's 'er trouble.'

'She's pregnant.'

'Eh?'

'She's pregnant.'

'Is that why she wears them pinafores?'

'Yes. So if she come out of the house and trips over your dustbin and has a miscarriage, I'll know who's responsible. Good night and God bless you and make you a better woman. Amen.'

'Amen yourself.'

He went upstairs and found Angela in the kitchen washing up the breakfast, lunch and dinner dishes. Even bent over a steaming sink, she managed to retain a look of freshness—a combination of angel and slut, he decided, and closed his mind to the contrast between these rooms and the ones he had seen in Brighton. He took down a cloth and began to dry plates, and she looked round in surprise, shook back a long strand of hair and gave him a welcoming smile.

'Didn't hear you come in. Want anything to eat?'

'No, thanks. I had a meal at Oliver's.'

'Not cooked by Henrietta, I'll bet.'

'Soup and steak from the restaurant. She wasn't there.'

'Lucky you. Tired?'

'I should be; I've hauled Mrs Major's dustbin back to its rightful place and explained that the lady's pregnant. When's it due?'

'In about five or six weeks.'

'I thought you were going out tonight.'

'I called it off. The hood of James Paynton's car leaks. Imagine being dripped on in weather like this!'

'Paynton? I thought you were going dancing with Bates.'

'No, thank you. I'm sick of him. And I'm sick of his schoolboy jokes. Like tonight, ringing up and putting on a peculiar accent and pretending to be an Italian called Potsy.'

The bowl that Rodney was drying gave a twitch and leapt from his hands, to break in pieces on the tiled floor. Mechanically, he bent to pick them up, and then rose and stared at his sister.

'What did you say?' he asked in a dazed voice.

She was stacking a pile of plates.

'I didn't say anything. I might have done, considering that that's the last of the Breton china. Don't look so worried; what's a bowl more or less?'

'I said—What—did—you—say?'

'I've just told you—nothing. What are you looking like that for?'

'WHAT DID YOU SAY?' He pulled himself together and spoke quietly. 'On the phone.'

'Oh, on the phone?' She eyed him uneasily. 'I don't see that it matters—'

'Before I strangle you, will you please tell me
106

exactly what was said?'

She twisted the cloth she was holding and spoke reluctantly.

'Nothing, really. He just put on this accent and said he was Signor Potsy. That's all.'

'And you said?'

'I said ... well, I can't remember, exactly.'

'Did he say any more?'

'Well, he said: "This is important. I am Signor Potsy..." and I, well, I...'

'You hung up?'

'Yes. No. I said...'

'You said?'

'I said if he wanted to be really impressive, he should have chosen a better name than Potsy. And then I ... I rang off.'

He hung the cloth very carefully over the stove to dry, and then glanced up at the clock on the wall. Eleven-thirty. Too late; accountants needed their sleep. He walked past Angela and out of the kitchen. After a moment, she heard the door of his room close quietly.

CHAPTER FOUR

When he had finished breakfast on the following morning, Rodney went to the telephone to put in a call to Signor Piozzi. Then, feeling that it was too early, he decided to make a personal call instead. By the time he had got to Park Lane through the rush-hour traffic, the Signor—he hoped—would be through his bath and breakfast.

When he arrived at Madame Landini's house, his request to see the Signor was forestalled by an invitation to enter. Led along the broad corridors, he felt relief at being back in the first-class section, but was he on his way to Signor Piozzi or to the Maharajah? He was ushered into a lift, taken up one flight and then followed his guide along a gallery that overlooked the entrance hall. At the end was a double door. The guide knocked; the voice that answered was Madame Landini's. The next moment, Rodney found himself standing at the edge of a pale green ocean of carpet; on the farther shore, reclining on a sofa, he saw Madame Landini. She gave him a languid smile, held out a hand, and as he drew near told him in a weary voice that she was very glad he had been able to come; would he please sit down for a few minutes? She had something to say to him.

He sat down and tried to decide whether Signor Piozzi, finding that last night's summons had misfired, had put in another call after he had left the house this morning. Before he could make a guess, Madame Landini had begun to speak.

'I will tell you,' she said, 'why I asked Signor Piozzi to telephone and ask you to come and see me.'

On his entrance, he had felt that the invalid pose was slightly overdone, but now he could see that she looked almost haggard, and she had lost something of the arrogance that had characterised her during the negotiations for the publication of her memoirs. Not all the ribbons and laces of her morning robe could draw his eyes from the signs of age and fatigue on her face. It was with genuine sympathy that he asked whether she was feeling better.

'You are very kind. Yes, I am feeling a little better,' she said. 'I must rest, of course, but I feel stronger. May I tell you why I sent for you?'

'Please do.'

'I wish the secretary, Miss Baird, to return.'

'I see. I'll do my best—'

'That is, if she will. You will arrange it?'

He caught himself up on the point of saying that he had already arranged it.

'It might be difficult,' he said instead, 'if she has taken another job.'

'There will have been no time for that.'

'Perhaps not. I'll do my best. She doesn't live in London.'

'Yes, she does. She told me that she has rooms, a room.'

'She gave it up and went home.'

'Where is her home?'

'Brighton,' he said, and at once wished that he had made it Boscombe or Bognor.

Brighton, he remembered too late, was at the very head of Madame's list of banned towns and cities. The list was not a long one, but once a name was entered upon it, it was never removed. Whenever and wherever she had consented to give a concert, she expected, and was invariably given a royal reception. If—as had happened at Brighton—an unfortunate official or civic dignitary omitted the smallest detail of the ceremonies, the concert was immediately cancelled and the place never again visited. It was a pity to have brought up Brighton now.

But he could see only a faint frown on Madame Landini's face.

'Brighton is not far,' she pointed out. 'If you go today, you will be there before she has time to arrange another post. You may tell her that I regret very much my words to her. I was of course ill.'

'If she's free, and can return, when would you—'

'At once. And one thing more; two things more. First, I would like her to consider the post a resident one. I was about to ask you this when you said that she had given up her room; perhaps this will make it simpler. If she refuses, as she refused before, I will not insist. The second, the last thing, I will give no guarantee that I will resume my memoirs. I wish to, naturally, but my doctor says that I am to do nothing strenuous, and as you know, writing

110

them is not a light task. The fact that Miss Baird is here in the house means that from time to time, as I feel like it, I can dictate notes to her. If I do not feel up to this, she can perform other duties; she could perhaps help Signor Piozzi a little. He has a great deal to do; he has arranged the sale of some of my property to His Highness, and he is also going to arrange schools for His Highness's grandsons—they are to have, as he had, an English education. And now, will you forgive me if I dismiss you? It always gives me great pleasure to see you, but at present I am not up to talking. Will you be so good as to ring?'

He rang, was shown out and drove to the office to make a report to Claudius and Phoebe.

'Of course I'll go down to Brighton and fetch her,' he said, 'but what do you suppose Madame's idea is? If she doesn't start again on her memoirs—'

'Of course she'll start again,' Phoebe prophesied with confidence. 'She doesn't want to commit herself, that's all.'

'I think I agree,' Claudius said. 'Once the girl goes back, I'm sure the book will go on.'

'I can't see her taking the job back unless she's allowed to live out,' Phoebe commented. 'She's the independent sort, and she's felt Madame's claws. Rodney, you'd better see if her old room's free, just in case.'

'It isn't.'

'Then find another. Or perhaps she'll suggest a place when you see her. And don't drive too fast on these dangerous roads.'

'See you tomorrow,' Rodney said from the door. 'No, tomorrow's Saturday. See you on Monday.'

It was almost as bad weather for driving as yesterday had been; there was snow at the beginning of the journey and coastal fog at the end. He stopped once on the way, and made two telephone calls. The first was to Oliver, to put him in touch; the second was to his sister.

'Angela?'

'Oh, it's you. Did I muck up anything last night, Rodney?'

'No. Listen; I've got some orders. Can you hear me?'

'Orders, you said.'

'And meant. Look, Angela, you've got to clear out that third bedroom.'

'The ... But I can't! It's crammed with stuff, heavy stuff. I can't lift it.'

'What you can't lift, shove. It's mostly empty trunks and suitcases. Shove it all in the junk room.'

'The junk room's full of Mrs Major's ghastly bits of furniture—you know it is! That's why we moved the trunks and things into the spare bedroom in the first place. And as well as trunks, there are all those books, and the wine from Spain that you bottled, and the carpets that don't fit, and—'

112

'Get it all cleared out, air the mattress and put down the rug from my room and hang up some pictures and then—are you there?'

'Yes, I am.'

'Go round with the vacuum cleaner—round and underneath too—and get the place tidied up and clean. C-l-e-a-n.'

'But I can't—'

'Get Mrs Major to help you, and have the place looking like a Home Exhibition by the time I get back, which'll be around five or six. Got that?'

'Yes, but—'

'Good.'

He rang off and continued his journey. Brighton, when he reached it, had yesterday's deserted, woebegone look, but his mind was on other things. He drove to the road behind the *patisserie* and stopped at the garage to see if the van was inside. In. She might be in, too. He walked round the corner and pressed the bell of Number 12A. There were swift footsteps on the stairs—certainly not her mother's—and then the door opened.

'You again!' she exclaimed.

'I've seen Madame Landini. She sent for me. She wants you back.'

She motioned him inside and closed the door. He answered her questions as they went up the stairs.

'She's decided to go on?'

'She hasn't actually said so, but we feel that's

113

the idea.'

'Why me? Why not someone else, someone who hasn't seen her with her temper showing?'

'She said you.'

'I hope you remembered to ask for an increase in pay, to make up for the insults?'

'It would have been taking an unfair advantage. She looked ill.'

'When does she want me?'

'Straightaway, if that's possible.'

They were at the top of the stairs. Standing in the middle of the living room was Mrs Baird. She gave Rodney a brief nod, and spoke to Nicola.

'I heard. You're determined to go.'

Nicola went up to her, kissed her lightly on the cheek and then walked into her bedroom; leaving the door open, she began to pack.

'I'm not determined, I'm not even anxious, I'm not sure I'll stay,' she told her mother through an open doorway. 'But why break off in the middle? The fact that she's asked me to go back means that she'll be like honey and apologise every time she gives me some work to do. She's put herself in the wrong and it's a situation I ought to explore, correction, exploit. Mother, could you be an angel and make some coffee before we go?'

Mrs Baird went into the kitchen. Rodney went to lean against the door of Nicola's room, watching her. Neat in everything she did, he thought, and contrasted the beautifully-folded, beautifully-ironed garments she was putting into the suitcase with the rolled-up bundles which Angela stuffed in when she packed. Everything in this room was orderly—no clutter of snapshots, just two photographs, one on the dressing-table, the other on the bedside table.

'My father,' she told him as his eyes rested on them. 'Not handsome, as you see.' She closed the case and swung it to the floor. 'I'm ready.'

He carried it out and placed it near the stairhead; when he turned, Mrs Baird was placing a tray on the table.

'I've made sandwiches for your lunch,' she said. 'At the end of the week, the restaurants may be full.'

She poured coffee for them, but she would not join them; she went into Nicola's room to check that she had left nothing behind and then sat in a chair beside the table, listening, answering when an answer was required—but Rodney knew that her mind was elsewhere, struggling with a problem to which he had no clue. He saw, to his dismay, that her hands were clutched tightly together on her lap, the knuckles showing white. All this anxiety, he wondered uneasily, because her daughter was going back to a woman who had momentarily lost control and shouted at her? She hadn't objected to Nicola's living and working in London before she took the Landini job; why work herself up now? She couldn't be worried about his own appearance on the scene; he well knew that he was the red-haired, freckled, homely, harmless type warranted to arouse trust in the most suspicious parent. So it was not himself that Mrs Baird was worried about.

Whatever it was, she was taking it hard. This was worse, he reflected morosely, than the time he brought Angela up to London, leaving his mother to take the full weight of the quarter-deck routine. A feeling of pity rose in him and drove him to disclose a fact that he had meant to keep to himself until he and Nicola were on their way to London.

'There's one thing I haven't mentioned,' he said. 'Madame Landini wants Nicola to make this a residential job.'

'Residential job? You mean live in her house? Never!' Mrs Baird declared.

'That's right; never,' Nicola confirmed. 'I live out, or I stay here.'

'That's why I thought. So'—Rodney addressed Mrs Baird—'I asked my sister to get a bedroom ready—we've got three. I don't think Nicola will enjoy living with us—the rooms are cold and uncomfortable and we're not a tidy pair. But as Nicola had given up the room she used to have, I thought it might be a good idea if she stayed with us while she looked round.' He turned to Nicola. 'You'll like Angela, but she's not house-trained. I'm not much better. Will you try it?'

'Yes, thank you. What job does your sister do?'

'She starts her first job—travel agency—on Monday.'

She glanced at her mother, met Rodney's eyes, and rose.

'I promise to look after her, Mrs Baird,' he said. 'Here are all the telephone numbers—my house, Madame Landini, my office—so you can get hold of Nicola any time you want to.'

'Thank you.' Her voice sounded dull. 'Nicola, you've forgotten to take the sandwiches.'

'And my watch.' Nicola handed the packet of sandwiches to Rodney and went into her room. Her watch was not there, and a search revealed that it was not in the house and not down in the shop.

'Then it's out with the van. Mother, will you send it on to me?'

'No. I'll keep it until your next visit. Now hurry; you've kept Mr Laird waiting long enough. Take good care of yourself.'

The sun was coming through the fog as they began their journey. Nicola was silent, and he saw that she was frowning.

'Worried about going back?' he asked.

'No. I'm sorry my mother was against it, that's all.'

'Perhaps you mentioned the Maharajah and started her imagination working.'

117

'I didn't. Your uncle didn't say much about him, did he? Somehow, I got the idea that there was a lot more we didn't get to know.'

'Be thankful. Sometimes when you're talking to old people, you press the button marked Distant Past, and jerk them into reminiscences that go on, and on. And on.'

'I hope Madame goes on and on. Where did Landini's money come from?'

'Dirty deals, mostly—but long before Madame met him. By the time they married, he'd become a respected citizen.'

'Would you like to have multi-millions?'

'No. I want a smallish house, four children bright enough to win scholarships, a middle-bracket car and a decent little sailing ship. I've got the ship and the car, but the house might be a difficulty; it's got to overlook the Atlantic, so getting to the office will be a problem.'

'Does your father's house overlook the Atlantic?'

'It depends which window you're looking out of. It's on a promontory with an all-round view. Windy and wet, and no shops handy, but we all like it.'

They ate the sandwiches as they drove. Later, they stopped for tea at a café that did its best to make its customers feel they had slipped back a century. Rodney ordered cakes; after one glance at them, Nicola sent them away.

'What did you do that for?' he asked indignantly.

'Cake-mix,' she said contemptuously.

'How can you tell by just looking?'

'Not one of the things on that plate had ever seen eggs or butter. At the *patisserie*, we use— What are you ordering?'

'Hot toast.'

'Why not wait for dinner? I'll cook it for you—for you both. Or will Angela have done it already?'

'If she has, you'll wish she hadn't. If you stay with us long enough, perhaps you could give her a few cooking hints. She took a course before she came to London, but it didn't sink in. You might also try to stop her from cutting up my clothes.'

'Cutting up ...'

'My clothes. She does it to get a pattern for a replacement. Only so far, she's never succeeded in putting anything together again.'

She was silent. As he ate the toast, he thought he detected in her expression a faint shadow of apprehension. Perhaps he ought to have let her form her own impressions.

'Didn't you want to be naval, like your father?' she asked after a time.

'No.'

'What's he like?'

'Naval. He got up to Captain's level and then decided that he ought to retire and give more time to his family. From his family's point of view, it was a great mistake. None of us was the right material for being brought up to what he calls scratch. He kept trying. He still tries, at intervals, but not so hard. When I told them about the Landini memoirs, he and my mother dredged up a lot of memories of her, starting from the time the ship my father was in sailed up and down the English Channel looking for her first husband. They'd heard her sing and they never forgot it. They said she used to make people get to their feet and cheer until—'

'Did they mention the accompanist?'

'Why should they mention the accompanist?'

'You see? Vamp till ready.'

'You think he dived overboard, don't you?'

'I don't know. All I know is that if I ever go to sea with my husband, I'll have him roped to the deck.'

'Were you born at Number 12A?'

'Yes.'

'No brothers or sisters?'

'No.'

'If I'm asking too many questions—'

'Go ahead. If I think people are getting too probing, I invent answers. How old is Angela?'

'Twenty-four.'

'Does she like living in London?'

'I think so. It was her idea to come.'

'Does she go out a lot?'

'She could, but she doesn't. If I can't order any cakes, let's go.'

He had meant, on nearing River Street, to

give her a brief account of its recent history, but they were still talking of other things when he stopped the car outside the house. She broke off in the middle of a sentence to look along the rows of newly decorated houses, and gave an exclamation of surprise.

'This reminds me of that fancy mews your friend Oliver lives in. Which is yours?'

'This one.'

'Couldn't your landlady buy some paint?'

'She likes to look different.'

When he stepped into the hall with Nicola, carrying her suitcase, Mrs Major was going out, dressed in her best—and her best was good enough to prove that for the present, at any rate, she could live without selling her house. She stopped to greet Rodney.

''Ello, Rodney boy. Been to see where me dustbin is?'

'It's right outside the door.'

'An' now she's complainin' about me letting soapy water spill on the pavement. Some people is never 'appy. I've got to wash me front steps, 'aven't I?'

'If I slip on the soapy water, I'll see that you get a nice, long jail sentence,' he promised her.

'Got a friend with you, I see.'

'Miss Baird, who's staying until she finds rooms. Nicola, this is Mrs Major, who lives only to plague her neighbours.'

''E likes 'is joke. Just come to London, 'ave you, dear?'

'Just come back to London,' Nicola told her.

'An' where did you stay when you was 'ere before?' Mrs Major inquired, leaning on the banisters to enjoy a chat.

'I had a room near Pimlico.'

'Reely? I 'ad a niece once, livin' round there. Where was you, exactly?'

A glimmer of annoyance came into Nicola's eyes.

'Buckingham Mansions, Buckingham Street,' she said.

'You goin' to look for a job?'

'No. I've got one.'

'I suppose you're a secret'ry, or something like that?'

'No. A model.'

'You got any relations in London, dear?'

'No.'

'No parents, nor nothink?'

Nicola was climbing the stairs.

'No. I'm an orphan,' she said.

'You could call me that,' Mrs Major said. 'My old Mum died upstairs, in those very rooms. No brothers or sisters?'

'Yes. All in Australia.'

'I'll pop up for a chat one day,' Mrs Major promised.

Rodney put a hand in his pocket for his key and then decided to pound on the door. It was opened by Angela, in a long dress.

'Going out?' he inquired.

'No.' She addressed Nicola. 'You see, he

didn't tell me who it was he was bringing home, so I thought it might be the Italian whose phone call I ruined. Rodney hasn't told me who you are, either, but it's an easy guess: Madame Landini's secretary. Is she going on with the memoirs?'

'We don't know yet. We hope,' Rodney said.

He was at the door of Nicola's room, looking in. A nice job, he thought with gratitude; she really had worked hard to drag out all that lumber. It made a pleasant room: bedside table, his rug, books, pictures.

'This is lovely.' Nicola looked at Angela. 'But am I going to be in your way?'

'I'm only too happy to have you. Life with a brother can get pretty dull.'

'Give Nicola a drink,' Rodney said. 'I'm going to put on a couple more sweaters.'

He went to his room, tried to open the door and found it impeded by a heavy object. Pushing hard, he managed to get an arm in to switch on the light. After an appalled glance, he gave a howl of rage.

'ANGELA!'

She was in the living room, putting out glasses and talking to Nicola. She gave him an impatient look.

'Well, what?' she asked.

'What the hell did you shove all the stuff in here for?'

'Where else could I have put it?'

'I TOLD you. I said—'

123

'I'm not a weight-lifter. And Mrs Major was out, so I had to drag it all, and as the junk room was crammed, where else was there except your room? It's all the trunks and things,' she explained to Nicola. 'I needed a crane.' She held up a bottle. 'Can you drink this stuff? A man I know brings it sometimes—he's something to do with sherry.'

'I'll drink anything.'

'Don't say that again, or Rodney'll dish you out some of his home brew. Can you eat things out of tins? I was afraid to cook anything in case it went wrong.'

'If you've got eggs and cheese, I'll fix dinner. I'm an expert. Do you mind if I sit on the floor. I always do.'

'Terrible draughts come in under all these doors.'

'Rodney says you're going to work at a travel agency.'

'Yes. Office-boy. I assemble tickets and—Oh Rodney, do be careful. You nearly knocked the vase off that table.'

Rodney, transferring heavy trunks from his bedroom to the space he had cleared in the junk room, made no reply. He went on dragging and lifting, his fury increased by the attitude of the two girls, who appeared to have forgotten him. Having at last cleared his room, he washed off his sweat and most of his ill-humour in a hot bath. Coming into the living room in a sweater and old trousers, he saw the table laid and Angela carrying in a dish.

'The remains of my lunch fish, miraculously made by Nicola into mousse,' she told him. 'Salad coming up. Sit down and begin.'

He paused only to pour himself out a drink. Then he joined the others at the table; the mousse and the cheese soufflé that followed it were so good that he allowed himself to overlook the flow of culinary exchanges that passed for conversation.

The meal over, he explained that he had already done his share of work.

'While I'm here,' Nicola told him, 'I'd rather you stayed out of the kitchen.'

'Good. Don't hurry away.'

Left with Angela, Nicola referred to the visit she and Rodney had paid to Victoria Lodge.

'We saw your uncle,' she said.

'You don't mean he actually let you in?'

'Yes.'

'Did he show you the railway that Rodney says is so marvellous?'

'Yes.'

'I don't remember ever seeing him. Ever since the big row, he's kept away. Rodney saw him when he was living down in Brighton, and liked him. When Rodney likes anyone, it sticks.'

'I've noticed. Oliver Tallent, for instance.'

'Well, Oliver's a lifelong friend. We've all known each other all our lives.'

'Was he always the big bore he is now?'

'Oliver—a bore?' The tone made Nicola turn from the sink to give her a glance. 'Don't you like him?'

'If you do, I'll get myself fitted for glasses, to see what I've missed.'

'He's awfully nice, really he is.'

'So your brother keeps saying.' Nicola turned and began to help with the drying. 'How often does he drop in?'

'Here? Oh, never.'

'Old family friend?'

'Well, he's got his own circle of friends. I didn't see much of him at home after I was grown up, but since I came to live with Rodney, hardly at all. You can imagine what he thinks of this house, after his own.' She hesitated. 'I used to mind,' she ended, 'but I don't any more.'

'Doesn't he ever come to see Rodney?'

'Not here. They meet in clubs and pubs, and sometimes they team up and go out to dinner, but Rodney won't invite him here, I mean he won't give him a special invitation or press him to come—he'd rather die than let Oliver think ...'

'That's brothers. I used to think I'd like one—the girls at school who had brothers were always so popular. But what use are they, when you come to look at it? As now.'

'It doesn't matter much. I'm over it.'

'You are?'

'Well, I still think Oliver's nicer than any
126

other man I've ever met, either at home or here in London. Not that there were all that many at home, because my father was always around. He's one of those parents who've never caught up.'

'Caught up with what?'

'Oh, you know—men with long curly hair, hippies, hookahs, pop, pot, non-stop sex—in other words, life. The first time a man came to see me wearing a lace blouse and strings of beads, my father grabbed a gun and went out to shoot something—anything—to stop himself from shooting at the beads. Was your father like that?'

'From my mother's accounts, anything but. He died when I was five, so I can't judge, but in his photographs he looks pretty mild—benign. Are you looking forward to this job?'

'In a way. It's easy, that's one thing. I'm not bright. I couldn't even learn my way round the keys of a typewriter, and I can't spell, so that only leaves serving in bars and coffee bars, which I'd be no good at, or doing an office-boy sort of job. When I think what it cost to educate me, and what I'm good for, I feel I could have spent the money better myself.' She ushered Nicola into the living room. 'Shall we turn on some music?'

'Yes.'

'You do it while I wash my hair.'

Nicola decided to unpack first. When she went back to the living room, Rodney, outstretched on the sofa, was reading a manuscript.

'Noise bother you?' she asked, and getting no reply, started the music. In a few moments he looked up with a frown.

'You can keep that thing on, but turn it down,' he ordered.

'Certainly, Mr Laird, sir.'

A yell came from the bathroom.

'Can't hear.'

Nicola adjusted the sound, chose a book from the shelf and sat on the floor to read. After a time, Rodney closed the manuscript, dropped it beside the sofa, yawned and lay with his arms behind his head.

'Bed soon, for me,' he decided. 'Got everything you want?'

'Yes, thank you. Good night.'

He did not move.

'You're our first guest,' he informed her. 'My parents prefer hotels. Incidentally, Mrs Major's been re-engaged to come up and clean every day. That's what she used to do before Angela came, but Angela cut down the days to save money. Now she's planning to pay it out of her earnings.'

'Then I hope you'll give the money back and pay it yourself; she isn't going to earn much. From what I've seen of Mrs Major, a few hours of her cleaning won't make much difference.'

'She's a good worker. All the newcomers up and down the street would give their ears and whiskers to get her. Why did you tell her all those lies?'

'I told you. When people get over-curious, I start inventing.'

'Try and teach Angela the technique; the only item Mrs Major hasn't elicited about our family history is how much we weighed when we were born.' He gave another yawn. 'I've eaten too much. I'm not used to good cooking. If and when Angela gets a husband, he'll have digestive troubles.'

'Then I hope she gets your friend Oliver.'

His eyebrows went up.

'My God, women!' he said wonderingly. 'Ten minutes together over the washing-up, and they open their hearts. She actually told you about him?'

'I gathered she was hankering. If he's an old family friend, why couldn't he have been friendly?'

'Why should he? He saw her grow up. Maybe that accounts for his lack of interest.'

'When she came up to London, didn't he even ask her out?'

'No. At least, he asked us both out to dinner, and turned up with his current girl friend. I suppose you could call that making his position clear.'

'Why couldn't you have done something?'

'Me? What, for instance? Throw her at him?'

'There are ways.'

'Such as?'

'You could have given parties, and asked him here.'

'Here? It was probably seeing this place that made him keep away. It's been tidied up for you—we wanted to make a good impression, knowing your Swiss background. When Oliver saw it, it must have photographed itself on his mind. Why not forget Oliver and try to switch Angela to some of the other men who come after her? You don't like him, anyway.'

'She does. He seems to be the man she wants—she's had long enough to find out. I'm all in favour of people marrying when they've known each other practically all their lives—there aren't so many nasty surprises.'

'I brought the mare to the trough,' he pointed out. 'If all she's done is whinny after the one horse she can't hope to get, is it my fault?'

'Yes. And you've got it all wrong. She's the trough. Your job is to lead the horse to it.'

'The horse we're discussing isn't thirsty. I'd be interested to know whether you—'

He broke off. Angela, in a dressing-gown, her head in a towel turban, had come into the room.

'You two sound as though you're having a row,' she commented. 'What about?'

'Horses,' Rodney said. 'Which of you two female slaves will make me a nice, hot cup of cocoa?'

130

CHAPTER FIVE

Angela's job began on Monday, and ended on the following Friday, when her employer gave her two weeks' salary, a lift home and a promise to give her a reference, provided he had to put nothing down on paper. Then he left, remarking somewhat ambiguously that anybody could make mistakes.

Her mistake, she told Nicola and Rodney that evening, had been in failing to realise that there was more than one Washington.

'These two passengers, absolutely unconnected with each other, were both going to Washington,' she explained. 'An American came in to collect his tickets, and I naturally assumed he was going to *the* Washington—Washington D.C., if you know what D.C. means. I don't. So I put this man's tickets into a Washington D.C. envelope and gave them to him, and he went. Then this other American turned up to collect *his* tickets, and he was the one who was going to Washington D.C. but the other man had gone off with his tickets instead of the tickets for some quite different Washington, so there was a terrible row. How could I know about the other Washingtons?'

'Everybody knows,' said Rodney. 'Everybody except you. There's one in Georgia, one in Indiana, one in Kansas, one in

Ohio and—'

'If you're collecting them,' Nicola said, 'there's one in New Zealand, not to mention one in England.'

'That all came out when the row was going on,' Angela told them. 'They even wrote it down for me—Washington Pa and Washington La; imagine! Why couldn't they label them East and West and Upper and Lower? So now I haven't got a job, unless I take Jeffry Hodges up on that offer he made me once.'

'What offer?' Rodney asked.

'His aunt runs a boutique in Pont Street. He said he'd always put in a word for me, if I asked him—she's got a foul temper, and can't keep girls for long. I wouldn't mind how foul her temper was, if the money was good. Now that I've got used to working, I'd like to go on. I was taken out to lunch three times this week, a terrific saving.'

'Two week's pay for one week's work isn't a bad start to a career, if you've decided to have one,' Rodney observed. 'See if you can do as well at the boutique.'

He was aware that Nicola was less satisfied with the week's progress. He had been careful to ask no questions; if she had anything to tell him, he would hear it in time. But whatever she had done during the day, her evenings had not been wasted. Released early from Park Lane, and getting home first, she had brought about a noticeable change in the rooms. Mrs Major left the floors swept and the kitchen scrubbed, but it was Nicola who had made the curtains hang straight, who had strengthened sagging shelves and cleaned rugs and carpets, bringing to light designs which had been hidden for years. She worked without fuss. On the nights on which she did not go out, she cooked, washed clothes, ironed or sat contentedly on the floor, mending. Even Rodney's pyjamas had been made whole.

Her manner with the men who had come, on two evenings, to take her out, had been casual; she had been ready to leave, she had offered each of them a drink from her own supply, and had gone, returning early or late but making no disturbance on her return. One man was a doctor, the other a teacher at a boys' school at Brighton; that, and their names, was all Rodney had been told about them, but his eyes had informed him that they were in love, and he felt sorry for them because as far as he could judge, she didn't care whether they took her out, or went out without her.

She had on first coming raised the matter of paying for her room and board. Rodney had told her that this could wait until they knew what way the cat—Madame Landini—was going to jump. She had not argued, but every evening thereafter, there appeared on the table two bottles of wine—red and white.

On Friday evening, while Angela was

engaged in her weekend hair-washing session, she made her first reference to Madame.

'Nothing, so far,' she said.

Rodney, finishing a letter to his parents, raised his head.

'No mention of memoirs?' he asked.

'No. This'll depress you and I hate to say it, but I've got a feeling that something's snapped. I've been trying to figure out why, but the only conclusion I can come to is that she's like a lot of other people who start off with a rush—the thing wears thin, wears itself out, and they lose interest and pack up. For good.'

'Then why did she ask you to come back?'

'I wish I knew. Once or twice I've thought it was simply to make up for that display of temper or temperament—to erase it from my mind, as it were. She may have felt it was bad publicity to have an ex-secretary going round telling people what she looks like with her teeth bared.'

'Why are you so sure she won't go on?'

'I've told you. She seems to have forgotten her memoirs, if that isn't a contradiction in terms. She doesn't show any interest in her own past any more—only in mine; it's her way, I suppose, of being gracious. It's flattering, but it irritates me. I'd rather have her the way she was, outburst and all. I'm sick of being asked to join her at lunch or tea, or coffee in the middle of the morning. And I'm tired of answering her questions.'

'What does she want to know?'

'Nothing. It's just a general attempt to be friendly, but she's acting out of character; you can tell by the way Signor Piozzi looks at her every now and then, as if he hadn't suspected she had any maternal feelings. As I told you, I don't like personal questions unless people have a right to ask them.'

'Have you fallen back on inventing?'

'Yes. Go on with your letter. I'm sorry I interrupted.'

'Is the Maharajah still around?'

'He comes and goes. The *palazzo* deal's through. He now owns a mansion in Geneva, a *palazzo* in Venice, a villa in Antibes and a shooting lodge on several thousand acres of Scottish moor. All fully staffed. How poor old Signor Piozzi keeps track, I don't know.' She made a restless movement. 'I suppose I ought to be enjoying it. There's a lot to see, there's even a lot to learn. There are people in and out all the time, most of them weighted down with fame or money or titles, and some of them worth watching—but if she isn't going to work, I want to get out. I've got nothing to do but answer invitations and type lists of figures for Signor Piozzi. I'm not carping; I like the money. I don't suppose I'll ever be paid so much again, but I liked her better before she became friendly. I like my bosses to keep their distance. You said I wasn't to do any prodding, but if I don't, how will I ever get her back to her memoirs?'

'It would be fatal to try and push her. She's got to decide for herself.'

'I can decide for myself, too. I'll give her two more weeks; after that, I'm through.'

The telephone rang and he got up and went to answer, passing Angela as she came out of her room. There was nothing to be gleaned from his conversation; he said Yes several times, and then rang off.

'Who?' she asked.

'Oliver.'

'Oh. Work?'

'No. He wants me to make a fourth at dinner next week.'

She made no comment until she was with Nicola in the kitchen after they had finished dinner.

'That's the first time he's ever done that,' she said dejectedly.

'Who's done what?'

'Oliver. He rang up here to fix a party. Before, he's always had the decency to ring Rodney at the office. Don't think I mind not being asked—it isn't that.'

'I wish you'd put him out of your mind, and go out with those other men who keep ringing up.'

'I do go sometimes—you know I do. But it doesn't work. When I go out to dinner and look across the table, I have to take off the head of the man sitting opposite, and put

136

Oliver's on instead; that's the only way I can manage to look interested.'

Nicola pulled down a cloth from a hook and turned to look at her.

'What on earth made you fall in love with him in the first place?' she asked.

'Well, have you ever seen anybody better-looking?'

'Yes.'

'Or better-dressed?'

'Good-looking, and dressy. What else?'

'Nice manners; not off-hand, like so many of them. But it's no use. This Henrietta's really got him hooked. Someone told me that she and Oliver gave a party at his house the other night, and when he came home from the office, she discovered he'd forgotten to order flowers, and she made him go straight out again and buy some. I didn't think he'd ever take orders from anybody, least of all from her. You have to admit she's clever; everybody says so. And I can't even hold down a job.'

She went to work in the middle of the week as saleswoman at the Pont Street boutique. Her nightly bulletins to Rodney and Nicola stated that far from finding the proprietress bad-tempered, she found her very easy to get on with—so that her surprise was the greater when on Friday evening she was handed two weeks' salary and requested not to return.

'But you must have done something to upset her!' Rodney expostulated.

137

'I can't think of a single thing I did or said that could have annoyed her. She probably had someone else coming, and wanted to get rid of me. She can't have minded my telling customers when I thought a dress didn't suit them. If a woman with a behind like the stern of a battleship tries on something fringed that makes her look like a Madam in a wild west movie, it's only kindness to tell her so, isn't it?'

'Four weeks' pay for a week and a half's work,' Rodney summed up. 'Where do you think of going next?'

'How do I know? I suppose I'll find something.'

'Why don't you go to the agency I came from?' Nicola suggested. 'They're good; they'll find you something.'

Following this advice, Angela called at the agency on Monday, and in the evening produced a long list of vacant situations.

'Who told me there was an unemployment crisis?' Rodney asked in wonder.

'Nobody'd take any of these jobs if they really had to earn a living,' Angela told him. 'They're all down at lift-boy level, where I belong. Those aren't salaries; they're tips. If I weren't being boarded and lodged by you for free, how do you imagine I'd even be able to eat?'

She went through the list with Nicola after dinner. Rodney, on the sofa, finished a manuscript, dropped it on to the floor beside him and lay listening idly to the names of firms varying from lawyers' offices to linen-drapers. Soon he was asleep. When he awakened, the choice had been made. On the following Monday, Angela was sent for an interview to a firm in Knightsbridge, engaged and told to report for duty on the following day. She got home late from the interview and went hurrying to her room to change.

'Pour me out a drink, Rodney,' she called. 'I'm dining out, and I'm late, and Freddy Pearce'll be here in a minute.' She raised her voice. 'Nicola, I got the job. I've got to start tomorrow.'

'Where's he taking you?' Rodney inquired, carrying in the drink.

'That new Asian place. Curry. Oh God, there he is!'

Down in the street, a car horn was giving a prolonged signal.

'A bit more of that,' Rodney said, 'and Mrs Major'll go out and say a few words.'

'Tell him to come up, will you?'

'What, Freddy Pearce? I certainly will not. Last time I asked him to come up, he got through three whiskies before you were ready to remove him.'

She finished changing in record time, and went out struggling into her coat. The door banged.

'I forgot to ask her where the job was,' Rodney said.

'They must be hard pressed, if they took her on in the middle of the week. Well, let's hope it takes her mind off Oliver. I think she's lost him for good.'

'She knows,' Nicola said.

'Has she heard anything definite?'

'No.'

'She soon will. Henrietta's called up reinforcements.'

'What sort of reinforcements?'

'I made a fourth at dinner. The other three were Oliver, Henrietta ... and Henrietta's mother. She's come all the way down from Scotland, bearing—like the youth in the song—

... through snow and ice
A banner with a strange device.

The device means: Marry my daughter.'

'That's what he wants to do, isn't it?'

'Judging by his tone when he asked me to make a fourth, and by his far from festive demeanour at the table-for-four, I'd say he didn't want to do it at all. He looked anything but happy.'

'Good.'

'Surely you don't dislike him enough to want to see him tied to Henrietta, do you?'

'They'll make a good pair. What makes her think her mother's going to be any help?'

'She's not meant to help. She's meant to

hinder Oliver from making his getaway. Poor Oliver.'

'Poor Angela.'

'She's got her career. Watch her come home on Friday with the sack and two weeks' pay.'

But on Friday, Angela was still employed. Coming home and announcing the fact, she changed into a new trouser suit which she said was the first expensive thing she had ever been able to buy with her own money.

'Like it?' she asked Nicola.

'Yes. Going out in it?'

'Yes, to the Bates' party. Oliver and his girl friend are going to be there, and this time she won't be able to look down her nose. Didn't you say you were going to a show?'

'I was. I decided not to.'

'So some poor chap's stuck with the tickets,' Rodney said.

'No, he's not. He gave them back and got his money back and went back to Brighton.'

'Oh, it was that one, was it?'

'It was.' She paused, studying him. 'I've been here—how long?—and you've never taken out a girl. What's the matter with you?'

'Tell her,' he asked Angela.

'There's a lot to tell. Where do I begin?'

'Begin with money. To take a girl out to dinner takes about half my month's salary.'

'Why can't you go somewhere cheap?' Nicola asked.

'Because there's something about the girls I

meet that makes them suspicious of being taken somewhere cheap. They think I'm undervaluing them. There's the beer-and-sandwich routine, but I've never found it helpful in stirring a woman's passion.'

'How about those girls,' Nicola asked, 'who live in nice apartments, who invite you and cook you a meal?'

'I don't like being taken home and cooked for.'

'Then why not bring her here, and make one of your omelettes?'

'He tried that with three different girls,' Angela explained. 'I wasn't living here for the first two, and I absented myself tactfully when he brought the third, but—'

'The first girl,' Rodney recalled, 'spent the evening shivering and complaining about the lack of heating. The second had an argument with Mrs Major after she'd nearly knocked her down with her car. The third—'

'—drank too much of Rodney's home brew and took off all her clothes and danced on the landing. Rodney didn't mind, but I happened to come back too early, bringing Austin Bates, and—'

'—and there he is, hooting. Go down and intercept him on the stairs and take him away,' said Rodney.

She went out. They heard the car driving away.

'What's this job she hasn't been thrown out

of?' he asked.

Nicola answered absently. 'Packing department. They give her the orders and she packs the things in a box and sends them off.' She raised her eyes to his. 'I want to talk to you.'

He poured drinks for them both and carried them to the sofa.

'You're on edge,' he said. 'I've been watching you. You're going to give up the job, aren't you?'

'I think so. But that isn't what I was going to say.'

'Then—?'

She sat silent, and he did not disturb her. At last she put a question.

'You don't know me very well, do you?'

'Oh yes, I do. I've been making a study of you.'

'In that case, perhaps you'll agree that I'm not inclined to let my imagination run away with me.'

'Has it tried to run?'

'I'll let you judge. Here's how it goes, from the beginning. Ready?'

'Yes.'

'I told you, didn't I, that Madame Landini had given me a room—'

'—to leave your things in. Yes.'

'I don't use it much. I hang up my coat, leave my handbag there, and my shopping parcels, if I've done any shopping. This week, someone's been going through everything I left there.'

He thought it over.

'Servants?' he suggested at last.

'No. I thought it might be, but my money wasn't touched—and why should they steal money? They're all probably a good deal better off than I am, and if they want to steal, why not start on Madame's things? Besides, this room is just down the corridor from Madame's suite, where she spends most of the day—there are people going in and out quite a lot of the time, so I don't see how any servant could have got into and out of my room without being seen.'

'You're sure no money was taken?'

'Quite sure. And I'm sure that my handbag was turned out—more than once. I don't know how I first became sure—you can't explain how it is that you suddenly realise that things have been moved. But today, I made up my mind that I'd try and prove it. I left everything looking as though I'd just put it down naturally, but I checked exactly where every item was. I had lunch down in the office—it's a sort of rule now that I have it with Madame when she hasn't got guests, but today she had. When I got back to my room, I knew somebody had been through my things.'

'And nothing was missing?'

'Nothing. But my mother's last letter, which was in my handbag, had been taken out of the envelope—and put back again. You said I was edgy. Now you know why. I'd understand it if something had disappeared—but nothing has.

Nothing I have is of the slightest value or the slightest interest to anybody except myself, so when someone's been examining my things, I get a funny feeling. Wouldn't you?'

'Yes. If you rule out servants—'

'I do. I think it's Madame Landini. In fact, I know it's Madame Landini. Want to know how I know? Guess.'

He hesitated.

'Scent?' he hazarded.

'Right. You can't mistake it. It's probably the most expensive scent on the market, so it doesn't exactly hit you. It's what they call subtle. It's so subtle that it's almost not there. It's just a faint breath in the air—but it's Madame. I ought to know; I've been with her all day, in several rooms of the house, for weeks. Nobody, none of her maids, would dare to use any. So it's Madame who's been searching my bag and my pockets, and reading my letters. So she's either crazy, or she's after something. If she's after something, what sort of something?'

'Evidence that you're typing something about her, to use in the future?'

'Why should I type it in her house? I've got free evenings. And what could I use that isn't already in her memoirs, as far as they've gone?'

'She broke off just before she came to Landini. Could there be—'

'—anything about him she doesn't want known? If there had been, she could have

145

locked some of her papers away. I've had free access to them ever since I went to work for her.'

'Apart from going through your things, does she seem odd in her manner?'

'In the way I told you, yes. It's that attempt to get friendly. It's ... it's forced. So if you don't mind, I'm getting out. I'm sorry, because I know you want her to go on with her memoirs, but I'm pretty sure she isn't going to. Ever since the big row, she's been ... different. I don't think she's well. So if she doesn't get back to normal and start work next week, I'd like to get out of her house.'

'All right. I won't say anything to Claudius.'

'I'd rather you didn't say anything to anybody. To people who didn't know me as well as you claim to, it would sound ... well, you know how it would sound.'

'You took the job to type her memoirs; if no memoirs, no job, if no job, no need to stay. And now stop worrying, and get up. We're going out.'

'Out? Dinner's in the oven.'

'Switch it off. We'll have it tomorrow. Tonight, we're dining out. You haven't been having enough change, and the job's gone stale on you. Why do you turn down invitations so often?'

'If I wanted to go out, I'd go out.'

'Well, you're going out now.' He went into the kitchen and turned off the oven, came back

146

and pulled her to her feet. 'Come on.'

'Where are we going?'

'Somewhere I can guarantee they use real eggs and butter.'

When they were in the car, he turned in the direction of Greenwich.

'How's your history?' he inquired.

'English, French, Biblical—?'

'Local. The history of the place you're living in. How much, for instance, do you know about Deptford?'

'Nothing.'

'Haven't you tried to find out?'

'I can see I'm going to find out now. Proceed, Professor.'

'Didn't you even know that Drake's ship, the *Golden Hind*, was docked here in Deptford?'

'No.'

'Did you know that Samuel Pepys trod the streets we're driving through now?'

'No.'

'I don't believe it. Even Angela knew that. The very air round here is full of England's great past, and what do you care? How much do you know about Greenwich, towards which we're now heading?'

'Everything. The Naval College.'

'And—?'

'There's more?'

'More? More? The Saxons gave it its name: Grenavic, meaning green village or town. The

147

Danes used it as a base when they sacked Canterbury; they burned the Cathedral and brought Archbishop Alphege back to Greenwich in chains. The year was 1011. I can never understand why the film-makers don't use episodes like this, instead of the tripe they dish out. The Archbishop's ransom was fixed at three thousand pieces of silver, but he wouldn't let his needy people pay it. The Danes killed him seven months later, in spite of the appeal of a Viking commander by the name of Thorkell the Tall. I wouldn't mind using Thorkell as a name for my son. He offered everything he possessed, excluding only his ship, in return for the life of the Archbishop, but his appeal was turned down and the Archbishop was killed.'

'There's a church—'

'You're waking up. St Alphege's, said to be built on the murder site. To skip a century or two; when Henry the Fifth returned in triumph from Agincourt, where did the Lord Mayor of London and the Aldermen and four hundred citizens meet him?'

'Greenwich.'

'Wrong. They met him at Blackheath, which we're now driving through. It was Henry the Fifth's brother, Humphrey, Duke of Gloucester, who built the first real palace at Greenwich. I'm going to write Humphrey's biography one day, but we'll skip it for now. I suppose you know that Henry the Eighth was born at Greenwich? So were his daughter Mary, and the great Tudor Elizabeth. It was at Greenwich that Elizabeth signed the warrant for Mary Queen of Scots' death. Are you beginning to soak in your surroundings?'

'Yes. Why didn't you write about all this, instead of about war in Napoleon's time?'

'I did think of it, but there seemed to be so much too much. I've settled for Humphrey. We're now going to drive to the Isle of Dogs and look across the river at the magnificent panorama of the Naval College and the Queen's House. After that, we'll drive to a nice Swiss restaurant I happen to know.'

The entrance to the restaurant was not prepossessing—a shabby doorway giving on to stairs that led down to a basement. But the room was large, warm and quiet; the food was good, the service friendly and the waiters Swiss.

'Which is why I brought you,' Rodney explained. 'To show off your French or German or both. I used to come here before I discovered I couldn't afford to take out girls.'

He paid the bill without pain, for the two bottles of wine, and the brandy which accompanied their coffee, had been presented with the compliments of the Swiss manager. He had done his best to keep up with Nicola's consumption of the free wine, but found it difficult. He listened with some reserve to her claim to have a head as hard as the table, and

149

was not unduly surprised when on settling herself in the car for the journey home, she gave a deep sigh, leaned slowly against him and fell into a sound sleep. How sound it was he did not discover until he had stopped the car and tried to rouse her. Backing out of the garage, he opened a window and let in a current of icy air; she slept on. He tried slapping and shaking; shouting was impossible, since he was afraid of disturbing the neighbours. He drove to the house and sat wondering how he could get her up the stairs. Much as he would have liked to, he could not leave her in the street.

He got out, opened the front door and propped it open with the dustbin lid. Then he went back to the car and forgot the problem of getting her up in the more urgent problem of getting her out. Finally, he turned her round in the seat, got her feet out, gave a tug and caught her before she hit the pavement. Thereafter, it was a matter of lifting her up and half-carrying, half-dragging her up the steps, across the hall and up the flight of stairs. He would have said that he was in good physical shape, and she was not an unduly heavy girl, but by the time he reached the landing, he understood why stage heroes seldom carried heroines, leaving this feat to their film counterparts and trick photography.

He got as far as the drawing-room sofa, and dumped her. She lay relaxed and flushed, like a schoolgirl with a temperature. He went into her room, took a blanket from her bed and laid it over her. Then he went thankfully to his own bed. His sleep was not restful. A crazed Madame Landini was at his desk, searching frenziedly through its contents.

On waking, he pursued the theme. Doctors could sometimes be right. A breakdown had been diagnosed, and this might be a symptom. If so, there was no use hoping that the second half of the memoirs, if they were ever written, would be equal in lucidity or literary merit to the first half. He was prepared to believe that people like Madame Landini were seldom completely normal; it must be almost impossible for anybody, man or woman, to support indefinitely the weight of spectacular success.

But he could not, as yet, bring himself to admit that there might, after all, be no memoirs. The gift had come unasked; he could not believe that it was about to be snatched away.

The house was quiet. He got up, put on a dressing-gown and went into the living room; it was empty. Nicola's door was open, her bed made and the room tidy. He looked into Angela's room and found her still asleep. Putting coffee on the stove, he heard the outer door open; a moment later, Nicola came into the kitchen carrying a bag of provisions.

'Good morning. How's the hangover?' he asked.

'It's fine, but next time you have to cover me up, use more blankets. I woke up shivering, and had to move to my bed. How are you feeling?'

'Fine. I didn't knock back the best part of two bottles of wine. Had breakfast?'

'Yes, but I'll make yours if you want me to.'

'Thanks. I'll go and have a bath.'

'It's a lovely day, with sun. I could hire your car and go down to see my mother and get my watch.'

'You could hire the chauffeur too.'

Angela appearing, they decided to take her with them. For the next half hour Rodney appointed himself time-keeper, and under his bullying the house was made tidy, the kitchen cleaned and the sandwiches packed, with five minutes to spare.

The sun, having made a token appearance, vanished. By the time they were halfway to Brighton, it was raining hard, but their spirits were high and rain could not damp them. They lunched in the car, parking it at a high view-point on the downs, and then drove into Brighton and called at Victoria Lodge. The gate was padlocked. Rodney climbed over it, and having knocked and got no reply, reconnoitred round the back of the house to satisfy himself that his uncle was not inside. They went on to Number 12A where Mrs Baird, notified by telephone, had prepared a substantial tea. It was a successful day, though

152

its object was not achieved, as Nicola did not get her watch; Mrs Baird told them that she had found it in the van with the glass broken, and had taken it to be repaired. They took her to dinner at a sea-front restaurant, and after leaving her at Number 12A, drove under a watery moon to London.

'Nice cheap day,' Rodney commented when they reached River Street.

'I paid for the petrol, but you paid for the dinner,' Angela pointed out.

'Wrong. I paid, and then Mrs Baird paid her daughter, who paid me. As I said, a nice cheap day.'

CHAPTER SIX

The following week opened at the office with an unprecedented pressure of work. Rodney calculated that this must be the first time in its existence that the firm had moved into top gear. Claudius was obliged to put aside his chess problems, and was seen wandering unhappily up and down the corridors in search of extra assistance. Phoebe could find no time for her usual Monday morning try-out of recipes from unpublished cookery books.

Claudius had a luncheon appointment. Phoebe offered Rodney soup and sandwiches in the kitchen, and he accepted. They did not take much time off, but when he rose to go back to his room, she asked him to wait a moment.

'Shan't keep you,' she said. 'I just wanted to say a word about Oliver. Do you realise he's looking peaked?'

'Piqued ... oh, peaked. No, I don't think I'd noticed.'

'You should have done. You might say it was love; it takes men in different ways. Some thrive on it and some wilt. He's obviously the wilty type, but what's puzzling me is why he's only just begun to wilt, when for as long as I've known him, which is about as long as I've known you, which is about three years, he's conducted a series of affairs with a series of women, and shown no sign of strain.'

'Well, I suppose—'

'Now don't go breaking in, I haven't finished. What I was going on to say was that although I don't particularly like him—I've told you so frankly, more than once—I don't want him cracking up in the middle of these negotiations over Madame Landini's memoirs. I shall sidetrack for a moment to ask if she has resumed them—has she?'

'No.'

'Then it's time one of us paid her an official visit. We can't be kept on thorns, can we?'

'I don't see what we can do. Nicola's there, ready to work.'

'She must by this time have formed some

idea of when Madame's going to get back to them; hasn't she?'

'She says there's been no sign. In fact, she's not going to stick it out much longer.'

'Why not?' Phoebe demanded angrily. 'She's being extremely well paid, isn't she? What makes these girls so ready to skip from job to job? Just as they begin to be useful, pfff! they've given notice and gone. Not to be married, oh dear no, I know it's not the thing to get married nowadays, and I only hope these licentious young women aren't going to end up as lonely old women. I've got no family, granted, but that's just my bad luck. I wanted a dozen healthy children and a husband who'd survive long enough to be a companion in my old age, to say nothing of doing half the housework and helping me on and off buses. I wish you hadn't started me on this. What was I saying before?'

'You were talking about Madame Landini's memoirs.'

'We've dealt with those. I said one of us must go and see her and ask her what she's about. What else was I saying?'

'You said Oliver was wilting.'

'That was it. Now, what I wanted to ask you was this: do you realise that people are saying he's actually going to marry this Gould girl?'

'I know the idea's beginning to spread.'

'Now what I can't stand, Rodney, is evasiveness, especially in you. I can see right
155

through you. Do you deny that you went out to dinner with Oliver, with Henrietta Gould and with Henrietta Gould's mother?'

'No.'

'There you are, you see? Why not say so at once? Stop being tiresome and trying to dodge. I'm simply trying to bring home to you some disturbing facts. One: I've known the Goulds for years, and although poor old Archie Gould didn't have an unkind bone in his whole five feet two, and never until the day he died ceased trying to manage his dreadful wife, she was and she remains a menace.'

'Well, I—'

'Two: her daughter has in the past repeatedly told people, in my presence, that she wouldn't dream of inviting her mother to come to London, because she would only be in the way. So why should she invite her mother at this juncture? You're not unintelligent; when you dined with them, you must have formed your own conclusions as to whether a marriage was being contemplated, or not?'

'Perhaps her mother came uninvited.'

'I happen to know that she came at Henrietta's request. Now, will you stop acting the court clown, and give me your honest opinion?'

'What do you want me to say—that he's caught?'

'If you think he is, why not say so? I'm not a gossip and I'm not likely to repeat anything you tell me.'

'All right, then. I think the combination of Henrietta and her mother is going to prove too tough for him to beat.'

'Is he in love?'

'He was. She's attractive.'

'She's a splendid-looking girl, I won't deny it. She's one of the handsomest girls in London. I won't say beautiful, because her expression's too hard—and pretty is too mild a word. But do you know, does he know, that she has a fiend's temper? At a party they gave recently, he forgot something trivial—flowers, I think it was—and she threw a book at him. Did you know that?'

'No. It sounds a bit exaggerated.'

'It isn't in the least exaggerated. I always check my sources. Now, it's nothing to do with me, but he's your oldest friend and so it's certainly something to do with you, and I advise you to get hold of him before it's too late, and have a little talk.'

'What good will a little talk do, if he's caught?'

'Good heavens above, aren't you his closest as well as his oldest friend? Are you going to sit twiddling your fingers while two scheming women get the better of him? I've no personal interest in him, but he's very useful to us professionally, and already I've noticed a slackness, a falling-off, a lack of zest in his work. So do something, and do it soon. And now you mustn't keep me talking any more; you're holding me up, and I'm really very busy.'

He put the matter at the back of his mind for the rest of the day, but it was of Oliver that he was thinking as he put his car away that evening and walked towards the house. As he went past Number 9, the door opened and the long, lank form of Peter Grelby stepped out.

'Saw you passing,' he told Rodney. 'I wanted to talk to you. First, I hope we're not running up your phone bill too much.'

'I hope so, too. How's your wife?'

'Oh, going along, going along, thanks. I say, Laird, something's really got to be done to control'—he paused to give a cautious glance up and down the street—'to control that old devil. The only one she'll listen to is you. Can't you do anything?'

'No.'

'It's getting serious, you know. I suppose you've heard about the air being let out of all our tyres?'

'No. When?'

'The first time, when there was that party up at Number 3. Eight cars. Thirty-two flat tyres. She couldn't have done it alone in the time; she must have called in some of those kids from round about.'

'How do you know she—'

'—had anything to do with it? Well, I mean to say, it does rather stare you in the face,

158

doesn't it? The only car that hasn't been tampered with is your own—see what I'm driving at? There was a suggestion that one of us ought to stay at a window all night, on the lookout, but nobody actually volunteered. If any of us try to say a word to her, all we get is insults delivered in words that a seaman would choke on. If you could get it home to her that there's such a thing as neighbourliness ... My God, here she comes. I'm off.'

Rodney walked on. He was almost at the top of the stairs when Mrs Major entered the hall. He leaned over the rail to address her.

'Been letting down car tyres?' he asked.

'No, I ain't. It's a lie. Try'n prove it. And wot if I 'ave? They was making that much noise, at that party, I couldn't 'ear me own telly. I suppose that chap from Number 9's been telling you. I've seen 'im sneak out of this 'ouse more than once. Wait till I catch 'im.'

'He was using my telephone.'

'Think I don't know? I use me eyes and me ears.'

'While he's my visitor, you'll lay off. Did you use your ears to hear that?'

'While 'e's yore visitor, 'e's upstairs. When 'e comes downstairs, I'll take a broom to 'im and sweep 'im clean off the doorstep, same's I did that pie-faced 'ouse agent wot came the other day. Anything else?'

'Yes. I've been asked to remind you that there's something called neighbourliness.'

'Oh, they've 'eard of it, 'ave they? Not a good morning' 'ave I 'ad outer any one of 'em since they came and ruined this street. You're the only yewman bein' among the lot of 'em, you and your sister and that orphan girl wot you've got stayin' with you. Why do they ask you to talk to me? What's to stop 'em from doing their own asking?'

'You've scared them.'

'I'll keep on scarin' 'em. Any more complaints?'

'Not at this moment. There's a nice smell coming up the stairs. Stew?'

'With dumplings. Light's a feather, in good beef gravy. Next time, I'll make some extra and pop up with a dishful. It's no use tryin' to teach that sister of yours 'ow to make 'em; she don't know the difference between shredded suet and soap flakes. Ta-ta for now.'

She opened her door and went in, singing. She had the remnants of a chesty contralto which, when he first came to live in the house, had been raised at all hours in militant hymns. Now, he knew, she sang only when she had brought off a successful coup against one of her neighbours. He let himself into the living room chanting seconds.

'On-ward, Christian so-ho-holdiers,
On to vic-tor-eeee.

Good evening.'

160

Nicola, laying the table for dinner, looked at him in surprise.

'You've got the wrong tune,' she said.

'That wasn't the tune. Mrs Major was singing the tune. I was making harmony.'

'So you thought. Did you remember to buy a paper?'

'No. Sorry. I was brooding over Oliver's troubles. Want a drink?'

'Please.'

'Wait till I get changed.'

He returned and poured sherry for them both.

'Costly,' he said, holding his glass up to the light, 'but worth every penny that Angela's boy friend spends on it. I think perhaps I'll go and live in Jerez when I retire. Where will you be?'

'Where my husband is.'

'Quite natural. The dinner smells almost as good as Mrs Major's. What're we having?'

'Roast mutton. There won't be any food smells after tomorrow; I've ordered a smell-extractor for the kitchen window.'

'Who's paying for that—Mrs Major?'

'No. You are.'

'It's her house.'

'It's your food smell.'

He was lying on the sofa. She was sitting on the floor with her back towards him, looking at the little fire. A stranger glancing in, he thought, would take them for a comfortable married couple: husband just home, meal

161

cooking, wife joining him in pre-dinner drink.

'Madame's still on the prowl,' she said, and her tone brought him upright. They weren't married, and trouble was looming.

'Tell me,' he said.

She spoke without turning. 'If I wasn't certain before, I'm absolutely certain now. It's her, for sure. She goes in while I'm at lunch and she goes through my handbag and she reads my letters. And I'm tired of wondering why. I've decided that she's suffering from some kind of mental complaint that a psychiatrist might diagnose, but which is beyond me. On Friday, I'm going to tell her I'm going. And before I go'—she turned to face him—'I'm going to tell her that I know what's been going on.'

'In the hope that she'll produce some kind of explanation?'

'No. I'll just tell her, that's all. I won't wait for the explanation. I'm not exactly scared, but ... Well, it's creepy.'

'If you're going to leave, leave, but don't stop to stir up trouble,' he advised.

'I thought of getting my mother to write a letter to me, saying she hoped I was wrong in thinking someone was reading my letters—but that would have started my mother going off her head. And I don't want to stir up anything. It's just that the whole thing's crazy. I told you that Madame probably didn't know what she was doing—but deep down, I'm certain that

162

she *does* know. I thought . . .' She broke off and ended on a note of finality. 'To hell with it.'

'*D'accord*. To hell with it.'

'I know what it means to you. I'm sorry. I would have liked to . . . Well, I'm sorry.'

'There's no need to be sorry.' His voice was quiet. 'I suppose I ought to have realised it wouldn't come off. There was always something phoney about it all—mansions and millionaires and Maharajahs. It was fun of a kind while it lasted. Don't let's brood.'

They sat in silence. After a while, she got up and took the glasses to the kitchen.

'You said you were brooding over Oliver,' she said. 'What's happened?'

'Nothing, except that Phoebe, who's known the Goulds for a long time, says that Henrietta's got a fiend's temper and throws heavy objects when upset. I'm to say something—to Oliver, not to Henrietta. I don't suppose you'll be sorry he's going to have a few things thrown at him.'

'I'm not sorry for him. Only for Angela. I still think that if you'd done something, anything, Henrietta wouldn't have got him. There isn't—'

She stopped; Angela was coming in. She was not with them for long; after a hurried change from a short dress into a long one, she asked Rodney to telephone for a taxi, and went out, with much grumbling, to attend an Old Girls' Reunion.

163

Nicola did not speak much at dinner, and refused his help in clearing up afterwards. She was still thoughtful when she joined him later in the living room. She sat in front of the fire as she had done before, but he changed his position so that he could see her profile.

'I've been thinking,' she told him.

'So I concluded. About Angela or about Madame?'

'About Madame. I was thinking that if she knows what she's doing—and I feel she does—then she knows she's looking for something. If she knows she's looking for something, it's something that she thinks I've got. She didn't touch any of my things when I was first working for her; this only began when I went back. So if there's a connection, it must be in something that she said, or did—or I said, or did—during the time I gave her the last sheets I'd typed, and her going out of her room and beginning to yell. Are you with me?'

'Yes.'

'Then try to believe what I'm saying. You don't see her every day. I do. Ever since I've been back to work for her, she's been different. I told you I thought it was because she'd had a kind of breakdown, but now I've had time to think, and to watch her, and I don't believe there was any breakdown. The only hallucination she's suffering from is this one about my having something she wants.'

'Shall we reconstruct? If we went through

164

exactly what happened between your leaving her in her sitting room, and coming out and seeing her on the landing, we might find a possible link.'

'We won't. Do you think I haven't been over it, and over it, and over it?'

'Let's go over it again—together. How long was it between your leaving her, and seeing her on the landing?'

'As accurately as I can fix it, eight minutes.'

'Time enough for her to have received a phone call that upset her.'

'No. I checked today. I couldn't check before, because I had to wait until I could do it without anybody knowing I was doing it. No calls go through to her room direct. And no calls were put through to her room during those eight minutes. There can't be any mistake. Every caller's asked to give a name, and the name and the time are noted in a book. I had a chance to look at the book for the first time today: no call. So we can rule that out. We can also rule out any possibility that there was something in those last sheets I typed that could have upset her—she read them while I was waiting, and passed them as all right for final typing.'

'Go over the eight minutes again.'

'I walked out of the room, waiting for a moment at the door because she asked me to keep a check of my overtime. Then I went to my room, put on my coat, put a few things straight—and then walked out on to the landing, or if you like, into the corridor.'

'That's too general. Take it from the beginning, slowly, trying not to leave out anything. Because if there's anything in your idea that you've some connection with all this, the reason must be buried in those last minutes you spent in the room with her.'

'All right. I knocked on her door. She said Come in. I went in. I handed her the papers. She was sitting on the sofa—well, half sitting, half reclining. While she was reading, I walked over to a window and looked out over the park. Then I heard her say there was nothing to be changed. I turned, ready to take the papers from her, but she seemed to want to keep them, probably because she sometimes liked to make marginal notes. She said there was nothing more I could do, and so I could go, and she was sorry she'd kept me late. Then she smiled, and got up and gave me—I told you—a condescending pat on the cheek and said we must be careful that I didn't overwork. I said good night and went to the door, and she said I must check the overtime hours, because I had to be paid for them. And I went out and closed the door and that was all. I don't think there was a single word said, apart from those ordinary remarks, all connected with the work I'd done.'

'Yet eight minutes later, she's out on the landing, yelling.'

'Yes. And what's so incredible is that we're sitting here looking for reasons, but the one who's really groping is Madame. I watched her closely today. She's got a ... I was going to say a questioning look on her face, but it's more than that. It's a probing look. She's trying to figure out something, and she thinks the something is connected with me. And if this doesn't sound too mixed up, I think she wants to get on with her memoirs, but can't, until she's got this thing sorted out. And I can't help her, and I don't like the feeling of tension, and I'm going on until Friday and then I'm leaving.'

'You don't have to stay until Friday.'

'It won't be too bad. The Maharajah goes and comes, and at the moment, he's around. He's drawn off some of her attention. The next person to stage a breakdown will be Signor Piozzi. They don't talk about *palazzi* any more, they talk about schools for the Maharajah's grandsons. All they say is "Guido, you will arrange this" and "Guido, you will arrange that." You liked the Maharajah when you met him that morning, didn't you?'

'Yes.'

'I like him too. I like the look in his eye. I like the look of him altogether. I get the feeling that if he clapped his hands, the room would suddenly be full of tigers or turbaned figures or beautiful girls in gauze pants. He gives out a kind of suggestion of ... of power.'

167

'Are you sure you want to leave the job?'

There was a pause before she answered. When she looked up at him, he saw that she had forgotten the Maharajah.

'Quite sure,' she said soberly. 'There's something wrong, and I want to get out.'

They said nothing more on the subject, but he found, during the next few days, that she had communicated to him something of her conviction that she was in some inexplicable way connected with Madame Landini's outburst. He thought of doing a reconstruction of his own for the benefit of Oliver, who came into the office to see him on Friday evening— but one glance at his withdrawn expression was enough to convince him that Oliver had troubles of his own.

Their business did not take long, but at its end, Oliver lingered.

'I was wondering,' he said, 'if you'd help me out again.'

'With Henrietta's mother?'

'Yes. It's not easy to pair her up at dinner. Older men find her a bit overpowering, and young men don't like being ... I don't quite know the word.'

'Hectored. I didn't enjoy it either.'

'I saw that. But you stuck it, which was wise. Some of the men I've asked to make up numbers get annoyed and answer back, and that breaks up the party.'

Rodney went across to take his coat off the

168

peg; it was as well to put the length of the room between them before putting his next question.

'What makes you think that Henrietta won't grow like her in time?'

He waited, but to his dismay, which grew greater as the silence lengthened, no reply came. His spirits sank. He had thrown out a challenge, as he had done so often in the past. Always, in the past, Oliver had taken it up. They had fought many battles—wordy battles, for even as a small boy Oliver had relied more on his brains than on his biceps. There had been no subject on which they had needed to hold back cards; only in the case of Angela had caution been necessary. Now he had spoken of Henrietta—and Oliver had nothing to say, and that meant that he was committed. Whether he was marrying because he wanted to marry, or because he was being manipulated into matrimony, didn't much matter; committed or caught, he was lost to his friends, because none of his friends would welcome or be welcomed by Henrietta.

When Oliver spoke at last, he had reverted to business.

'I went in and had a word with Phoebe,' he said. 'She's looking through the batch of photographs and letters that Madame Landini gave us. If we used them all, there'd be more pictures than print. Let me know what you think of them.'

'I will. I suppose she told you there's still no

sign of any further memoirs?'

'She doesn't take the gloomy view that you do. She says there's got to be pressure, by which she means that you, I, Claudius and herself will be sent in, in that order, to ... to hector her.'

'It won't work. How about meeting me for dinner one evening?'

'If I can manage it. Can you keep the thirtieth free?'

'Yes. Your birthday. Giving a party?'

'There's ... well, there's to be some kind of celebration. Henrietta hasn't decided exactly what kind.'

Oh yes, Henrietta has, Rodney told himself. He would have been willing to bet that she was going to use the occasion to announce her engagement to Oliver. Loud and clear and public, leaving him with no hope of escape.

'I'll make a note of it,' was all he said.

When Oliver had gone, he tidied his desk and went along the corridor to Phoebe's room. She was on the point of leaving; in her hand was the bulky envelope he recognised as the one containing the Landini illustrations. She handed it to him.

'I know you've seen them,' she said, 'but Claudius and I have just gone through them and I've made a few notes. You might take them home and study them during the weekend. Did you speak to Oliver just now?'

'Yes.'

170

'You did? Good. Did you make any impression?'

'No.'

'Then keep trying. I don't want to sound discouraging, but I think you've left it too late; there are rumours circulating about an announcement at the end of this month. Are you going out of town this weekend?'

'There was talk of a picnic tomorrow or Sunday.'

'Well, enjoy yourself.' They had reached the street and she was walking with her usual long, unhesitating stride. She never made way for anybody, however crowded the pavement; she merely marched, and oncoming pedestrians seemed to fall away, leaving her path clear. 'Mind how you drive. Do you know what the casualty figures were for last month?'

'No. Can I give you a lift home?'

'Thank you, no.'

'I practically pass your door.'

'So does the bus, and the driver drives more slowly than you do. Goodbye until Monday. Don't forget to look through those things. Which reminds me—isn't it odd how one can never really place any reliance on what people say? For example, that girl, Nicola Baird. I remarked on the peculiar watch she was wearing, and she told me quite positively that it was unique, and I believed her. Did she tell you it was unique?'

'Yes. It is.'

'It isn't. It's an interesting watch, and I don't suppose there are many of them around, but unique it is *not*.'

Rodney found that he had halted. Phoebe, finding him no longer at her side, retraced her steps in annoyance.

'If you can't keep up, I'll be getting along,' she said.

'What was it you said just now?'

'Just now? Nothing.'

'About the watch.'

'Oh, that? How can anybody hear anything when this traffic's making such a noise?' She raised her voice. 'I said the watch wasn't unique.'

'How did ... how do you know?'

'Because there's a photograph in that envelope of Madame Landini's first husband—what was his name again?'

'Anton Veitch.'

'That's right. Well, Anton Veitch is wearing a replica of that watch. Goodbye until Monday.'

CHAPTER SEVEN

There were times, Rodney realised as he drove homeward, when reason said one thing, and instinct sneered and said another. His reason told him that Phoebe must be right; there must be other watches of the kind that he had seen Nicola wearing. His instinct insisted that it was—as Nicola claimed—unique.

Before leaving the car park, he had emptied the contents of the envelope on to the seat beside him. There were letters and newspaper cuttings, but the greater part were photographs on the backs of which Madame Landini had written notes identifying the subjects. They showed her in childhood, in girlhood, on stage and off stage, alone or beside world-famous figures. Even if there were no memoirs, he had thought as he searched swiftly among them, the photographs would have made an absorbing book.

And then he came upon the photograph he was looking for. A man, standing alone on a terrace against a background of palm trees and white-flecked sea. A man dressed in linen trousers and sports shirt, clean-shaven, facing the photographer, leaning casually on the balustrade, his arms resting on it, one hand drooping negligently over its edge. Anton Veitch. Young, tall, handsome, grave. And on his wrist a watch, large, diamond-shaped, with a curiously-marked dial. A watch in every respect like the one Nicola wore, a watch she had stated to be unique, made in Switzerland at the beginning of the century and never duplicated.

A connection? Not necessarily, he told himself. Property owners frequently made false claims without knowing them to be false. But suppose ... The net of conjecture enmeshed him. Suppose ... suppose ... suppose...

He garaged the car and walked slowly to the house. She would have to see the photograph—but what would be the best way to bring it to her notice? He would have given anything to have been able to show it to her at once and say simply that she had been mistaken in supposing her watch to be unique, but he could not bring himself to accept this solution. He believed, and thought that she would continue to believe, that there was only one watch of its kind.

He entered the house with a sense of foreboding. In a way that he could not understand, the situation seemed to hold grave and even grim possibilities. He shrank from opening the door and facing Nicola with the envelope in his hand.

But when he entered, only Angela was at home. She was seated on the sofa, painting her fingernails.

'Hello, Rodney. You're late.'

'Not very. Where's Nicola?'

'She came in and went out again. She's dining with that man who came here to fetch her the other night. Not the Brighton one; the other. She left a pie in the oven.'

'Couldn't you put that lacquer stuff on in your bedroom?' he asked irritably. 'Why fill

174

this room with that smell?'

'You've never complained before. What's the matter—tired or something?'

Without answering, he opened a window, left it open and went into his room, taking the envelope with him. His mind was choosing and rejecting ways in which he could bring the photograph to Nicola's notice. He had decided against a direct approach; he wanted to give her time to study it alone, time to decide whether it had any significance.

He went early to bed. In his room, he took out of the envelope the four photographs in which Anton Veitch appeared. In three of them there were other figures round him. The fourth showed him alone on the palm-fringed terrace.

By the time he heard Angela put out her light, he had made his decision. He got out of bed, went back to the living room and left the four photographs on the arm of the sofa. If Nicola didn't see them when she came in, she would come upon them when she did her usual tidying-up of the room in the morning. He stepped back to satisfy himself that anyone entering from the landing would receive the impression that the photographs had been left lying carelessly. Then he went back to bed.

Putting out the light, he lay trying to make sense out of things that had no sense. When at last he fell asleep, it was to dream of Alsatians with bared teeth, Swiss coffee in blue cups, and Signor Piozzi bent over legal-looking

175

documents.

When he woke, it was still dark; for a moment he thought that he had slept only an hour or two. Then he saw the time—just after six—and heard somebody moving about in the kitchen. He got up, opened his door and went to investigate. He found Nicola, in jeans and a sweater, taking a pot of coffee off the stove. She turned to look at him as he came in, and he saw that her face was white and drawn.

'Hello.' Her tone was expressionless. 'Sorry if I disturbed you.'

'What are you doing?'

'Rub the sleep out of your eyes, and you'll see.'

He had not needed to rub the sleep out of his eyes to note, as he came through the living room, that only three of the four photographs were still on the sofa. She had seen and selected the one showing the watch.

'Look, Nicola—' he began.

She made an impatient sound.

'It's too early to think,' she told him, 'and it's too late to pretend. You left those photographs there for me, didn't you? You must have been studying the identity parade technique: line up a few and see if she picks the right one. When did you first—'

'Phoebe said you'd told her the watch was the only one of its kind, and the photograph proved it wasn't. Isn't.'

She put down her cup of coffee, untasted,

and faced him.

'If you agreed with her, you wouldn't have left that photograph there for me to pick up. You think there's a link missing, and so do I. You can't believe there's another watch, and neither can I. There's only one way to find out, and that is to ask.'

'If you're going down to Brighton, why didn't you wake me?'

'This isn't your—'

'Yes, it is. I'm driving you down.'

'I rang up and ordered a taxi.'

'We'll pay it off.'

He washed, shaved and dressed in ten minutes; he joined her and they went out of the house. The taxi was waiting; Rodney paid the driver. Then they walked round to the garage.

It was a settled, spring-like morning. He insisted on a brief stop for breakfast, and then she left him to telephone to her mother.

'What did you say to her?' he asked, on her return.

'Nothing except that you and I were on our way—this time without Angela.'

They did not talk much; it seemed useless to pose questions and supply probable answers when in an hour Nicola could put the one relevant query to her mother: how did Anton Veitch come to be wearing a watch in every way similar to the one she had stated to be unique?

'When did she give it to you?' Rodney asked

as they neared the end of the journey.

'On my twenty-first birthday. She told me it had been my father's, and she'd been keeping it to give me when I was twenty-one. It had been made by a famous Swiss watchmaker, she said; having made it and decided it wouldn't be a selling proposition, he didn't make any more like it.' She paused, and then put the question Rodney had been waiting for. 'Do you think the glass was really broken?'

He hesitated. After watching him for a moment, she spoke in a voice that had desperate overtones.

'Look, couldn't you come out into the open? It's frightening enough trying to sort out my own ideas. If as well as that, I've got to try and guess at the things you're thinking ... Because if the glass wasn't broken, and she said it was, then everything ties up—don't you see that? You said that the reason for Madame Landini's sudden attack of hysteria could be found in those eight minutes—and now we know you were right. Which shows you that however accurately I thought I'd reported, I'd left out the one vital item which makes all the rest hang together. I reported that she was sorry she'd kept me late, and I was to keep track of the overtime hours. How could I keep track of the overtime hours without looking at my watch?'

'You remember doing that?'

'Of course I remember, now that I know it's

something I should have remembered. I had on a long-sleeved blouse, and at the door, I stopped and pushed back the cuff and glanced at my watch. And she saw it—for the first time, because all the sleeves of my office suits are long. She saw it, and in the next eight minutes, she got into the state you and I are in now—ideas running round in circles, getting wilder all the time. She didn't dare to ask—how could she ask? When Anton Veitch was wearing it, he must have believed it was unique, and told her so, or she gave it to him, and told him so. All she knows is that he was drowned in the English Channel, so how could anyone steal the watch, and if it wasn't stolen, then what? I'm not surprised she yelled and told me to get out. And then she sat down and cooled off and realised that the only way to find out how it got on to my wrist, was to get me back and try to do some investigating.'

'But your mother—'

'Yes. My mother. Let's consider my mother. She came back from Switzerland and found out where I'd been working, and how I'd been thrown out. That upset her. I reported that too, didn't I, the first day I met you? But I left out another vital point, which was that when I came out of my room and saw her crying, she looked more than upset. She looked . . . scared. And then what? I go back to work for Madame Landini, but I can't find my watch. Here's another vital omission coming up: I could almost have sworn then, and I'll certainly swear now, that I left the watch on my dressing-table. But she found it in the van with the glass broken. She said. So those are the facts; now try and sew them together. I was trying to do that the whole night long. Now you try.'

'Your mother will—'

'—do the sewing?'

'Why don't you consider the most probable answer: that Anton Veitch wasn't wearing his watch when he went overboard?'

'If he wasn't, then we'll hear how it ended up on my wrist. And if it was my father's, why wasn't my father wearing it in either of those two photographs I've got of him? You've seen them. No watch.'

'Calm down.'

'I'm perfectly calm.'

'No, you're not. You're going to frighten your mother when she sees you. Why can't we stop and work out some way of ... She's not young. She ought to be given some kind of warning that this has come up.'

'That means giving her time to think, and suppose she thinks that it's better not to tell me anything, the way she didn't tell me anything before? She had time to think, while I was unpacking my suitcase and telling her how Madame Landini threw me out—and did she mention watches? No. I'm grown up. I know more facts of life than she ever did or ever will,

180

and I want to know the truth, even if the truth is that my father stole Anton Veitch's watch and pushed him overboard.'

'Your father was a—'

—'pastrycook, and they have pastrycooks on big liners, don't they?'

'I'm worried about your mother.'

'Well, I'm not. I'm worried about my father. She knows how he got that watch, and she didn't want to tell me. She guessed Madame Landini had seen it. She didn't want me to go back, and when I went back, she saw to it that I went back without my watch. If you don't want to stay in on this, if you'd prefer to keep out of it, just drop me at the shop and I'll meet you somewhere tonight for the return journey. I've got to go back. I was going to finish the job yesterday, as I told you—but I didn't. You can't give notice and make a speech to someone who isn't there. Madame Landini wasn't there. Neither was Signor Piozzi. Neither was the Maharajah. They all went out for the day, inspecting schools suitable for the grandsons of princes.'

'You won't have to go back there. I'll do all the explaining that's necessary. But while we're here, I'd like to stay with you. I'm as involved as you are. We both have to find out ... whatever there is to find out. But I don't like the idea of confronting your mother with that photograph without some kind of preparation.'

'Well, let's see about preparation when we get there.'

But when they reached the house, Mrs Baird was out. They went upstairs and Nicola's first action was to take the photograph out of the envelope in which she had put it. She placed it on the desk, took it up again, looked round the room and then propped it against a small carved box on a table in the corner.

'She won't see that when she first comes in,' she said. 'Then I can prepare her and ask her to take a look at the watch in the photograph. All right?'

'I suppose so. I don't like it. I think you ought to—'

'Here she is.'

Rodney waited. For the first time, fear touched him. Mrs Baird's secrets were her own, to keep or to reveal. There should have been a gentler, more gradual approach.

She was at the top of the stairs, and he stepped forward to take her shopping basket.

'Thank you. If you had only telephoned to me last night,' she said, addressing them both, 'then I could have arranged for—' She broke off abruptly, her eyes on Nicola. 'You are not well,' she exclaimed. She came forward and put an anxious hand on Nicola's forehead. 'You are very pale ... no, you have no temperature. What is the matter with you? You should have told me, if you have been ill. Come and sit here and tell me exactly—'

Her words died away. She had turned to pull forward a chair, and her eyes had fallen on the photograph.

For some moments there was total, tense silence. She took two slow steps towards the table, and they saw her hand go out and pick up the photograph.

Something—some instinct, some premonition—made Rodney retreat. He found himself moving slowly backward, step by step, until he felt the window behind him. Nicola had not moved. Her mother was standing motionless, frozen, her eyes on the photograph in her hand. Then she raised unseeing eyes and looked blindly round the room until at last her gaze fixed itself on Nicola.

'Where'—her voice was a whisper—'where did you get this?'

Nicola's face was deathly pale, but she answered steadily.

'Among the illustrations for Madame Landini's book.'

'And you brought it to me—here, to me?'

'Yes.'

'Why?'

'Don't you see? He was wearing my watch.'

The look of fear on Mrs Baird's face changed slowly to one of utter bewilderment.

'Watch?' she repeated uncomprehendingly. 'Watch?'

Nicola took a step forward, and then stopped.

'If you didn't notice the watch,' she asked in a shaking voice, 'then what ... then why ...'

'You wanted to find out if I—'

'All I wanted was to know why he was wearing that watch. When you gave it to me, you said it was unique. I think Madame Landini saw it, and I think that's why she stopped writing her memoirs, and I think you were afraid that she saw it, and so you made sure I couldn't take the watch back to London with me. The truth, that's all I wanted. Whatever was secret, I think I've a right to know. The truth, just the truth. I've been living for the past few hours in a fog, and I'm frightened. If you know anything, you ought to tell me.'

'I tried'—Mrs Baird's voice was hoarse—'I tried to prevent you from going back. You know that I tried. You wouldn't listen.'

She swayed, but before Rodney could move, Nicola had caught her arm and was placing her gently in the chair. Then she knelt beside her and spoke urgently.

'Mother, you've got to tell me. Rodney's in this just as much as I am. If you don't want him to talk about it, then he won't. But I've got to know the truth. Please, *please* tell me the truth.'

There was silence. Mrs Baird was breathing in short, painful gasps. Her eyes were closed.

'Mother—'

Her eyes opened.

'The truth? You want the truth?'

'Yes. All of it. *Please*. You ... you knew Anton Veitch?'

Mrs Baird spoke in a toneless voice. 'That was not his name, not his real name. He was an Englishman. His name was Anthony Vine.'

'When, where ... when did you know him?'

'He was my husband.'

'Your...'

'In the eyes of God, my husband.'

'If he ... if he was your husband, then...'

'Yes. He was your father.'

In the silence, Rodney heard the sound of the sea.

CHAPTER EIGHT

'His name was Robert Anthony Vine,' Mrs Baird said.

It was the same room, but to Rodney, it had changed. It had become the backcloth of a drama whose echoes had been sounding for the past weeks in Madame Landini's residence. Mrs Baird no longer seemed to him the same woman. Grey-faced, haggard, she was seated in a low chair, her hands in Nicola's, who was sitting on the floor beside her.

'His name was Robert Anthony Vine. He was English, born in Cheshire, the son of a clergyman. His parents had very little money. They died when he was a child; his only relation was an aunt, and he went to live with her. When it was clear that he had great musical gifts, his pianoforte teacher asked his aunt to provide money for his studies, but she refused—not because she did not believe in his talent, but because she herself was the widow of an unsuccessful musician, and wanted a more secure future for the boy. His teacher took him to London, and there he played for the great master Nikolaus Satz. It is from him that Nicola's name is taken. It was Satz who, when the aunt refused to pay anything, looked round for a patron—and found Princess Anna. She was young, but already world-famous, already rich, and she was known for her generosity to young musicians. She saw Anthony Vine, and heard him play.

'From that moment, she took charge of everything. She changed his name to Anton Veitch, she arranged his studies, she paid for his lodgings, his lessons, everything. She arranged his first concert. It was in London, and about its success, and the success of his three later concerts, there could be no doubt. But the future she had decided for him was to marry her.

'He was, of course, in love—how could he not have been? If she had been only beautiful ... but she was more, much more, and also she was an artist like himself. And above all there was his deep gratitude for all the things she had done for him. These he never forgot—as you will learn.

'They were married in New York. He was twenty-five, she was two years older. They went on a long honeymoon, and then they returned, as he thought, to resume their careers. And then she told him that she would never agree to be parted from him, never. As it was unthinkable that she should give up her own career, he must agree to give up his, and stay with her always, and become her accompanist.

'He told himself that he could not refuse to do as she asked. All that he was, he owed to her. So he agreed, and they travelled everywhere, and she sang. No recordings can ever be like that voice. Those who heard it ... it is true to say that they were lifted, for a time, into another world. I know, because whenever she sang in London, I went to hear her.

'In London, at that time, she and her entourage stayed always in the same hotel— the Regal, which was very old, and became out of date, and is now pulled down. A number of rooms, always the same rooms, were reserved for the Princess. In the basement of the hotel were the kitchens, and there your grandfather worked—a pastrycook, Swiss, of no account beyond his work, but in his own sphere an artist, a master like your father.

'I was his only child. When my mother died, he brought me over to England and I began to work under him. Soon he decided that I must

187

work in better conditions, that I must have more freedom, more movement, more change. I was put in charge of the flower arrangements of the hotel. Today, this kind of work is done by people from outside, who make a contract, but then, no. At the Regal, I did it. And one morning, as I was going into the Princess's suite, carrying a vase of flowers, your father came out.

'We met face to face. You must believe me when I say that from that moment, nothing was the same ever again, for him or for me. We knew, that first moment. We knew ... We passed, we looked round, we stopped, we spoke. That was how it began.

'We had to wait a long time to be happy. He had been married to the Princess for eight years. After the first year, she took lovers, but I believe, I have always believed that your father was the only man who really mattered much to her in her life. He was not happy with her, but he said nothing; always, always he remembered that he owed her everything and that it was through her that he had been given freedom to perfect his art. To the last, he refused to leave her in any way that would be known to the world to humiliate her. He would not have it said of her that her husband had run away.

'We waited for two years. The Princess travelled, and your father travelled with her. While she was in London, in the hotel, he did not always have to attend the receptions and the banquets to which she went; at those times, he was free. And it was then that we met. Anybody who saw me entering or leaving the rooms would think that I had gone there in the ordinary course of my duties; I had a key, I could go into and out of all the rooms of the hotel at will. In the little room at the end of the suite, a room that was your father's, in which he worked, practised, arranged programmes for the Princess's concerts—in this room we met. And loved.

'For two years, we planned. We were determined to make a new life together, but it could not be a happy life unless he left her in such a way that the world would not know he had run away. She did not need him any more, this much he knew, but he knew also that she would never let him go. So we waited. He and I would come together one day, and be happy— but the world must not know that he had deserted her.

'We knew that we would live here, in Brighton. It was a place to which she had stated publicly she would never return. We saved what money we could, but for him it was difficult, because all his earnings as an accompanist came through her, and she knew always what he spent. Soon, I came to Brighton and with my father's help I bought this house and started the *patisserie*. My father knew something, but not all. He knew that I was waiting ... for someone. I changed my name to Baird and told people that my husband was in a Swiss sanatorium but would soon be well enough to join me.

'And then he came. We had had time to plan; we did not make any mistakes. They had sailed many times from Southampton; he knew the timing, the routine, everything. The moment came when they were to sail to America on the *Atlantis*.

'He went on board the ship with the Princess. He stood beside her on the deck as she made her farewells to the crowds below. When the signal was given for visitors to leave the ship, he went down with some of her flowers to the stateroom. He left the flowers, put on a mackintosh, pulled a hat over his eyes—and went into the corridor. Now he was any tall man going ashore after saying goodbye to his friends. He was not so well known that there was any risk of being recognised. On the shore, he did not turn for a last look. He walked out of her life for ever.

'I was waiting here. My father had gone back to Switzerland. Your father and I began a new life, and he took a new name: Baird. He became Anthony Baird by law, and died Anthony Baird.

'We wanted children. You came, and we were glad; there were no more. As to his music, if you think that a man whose fingers had had magic in them could never be happy after abandoning his art, you are wrong. He chose, and he never regretted. I thought that perhaps he could teach others the piano, but he thought it was a risk, to bring music back again into our lives. So we lived quietly together, working in the shop. There was no secrecy, no anxiety and no fear. We earned enough to be comfortable, and we were content, loving each other.

'When you were growing up, I had to have photographs of your father to show you, but I could not risk giving you his likeness, because I thought that one day, you might meet someone who would recognise him. So I brought back from Switzerland photographs of my cousin Hans, who was the same age as your father, and who died at almost the same time. It is Hans whose photographs I put into your room.

'And that is the truth you wanted to find out. There is nothing else, except for you to try to imagine what I felt when you told me that you were working for Madame Landini, and she had dismissed you. You could not understand why, but to me, it was all quite clear: you had said that she asked you to check the hours that you worked overtime, and I knew instantly that you must have looked at your watch ... and that she must have seen it. I told you it was the only one made like that, and that is true. It was made by the father of Nikolaus Satz; he was a watchmaker, and when he was old, he amused himself by making some unusual

191

watches. This was one of them. In time it came to Nikolaus, and on the night of your father's first concert, he was so excited, so happy, he took it off his own wrist and put it on to your father's. Your father wore it always. So I knew what Madame Landini felt when she saw it. She felt fear.

'Yes, fear. On one point only was there disagreement between your father and myself—that was, whether she ever suspected that he was not dead. He said she did not, but for myself, I always felt sure that a doubt would remain in her mind. She must have known that he wished to be free, that he regretted giving up his own career, regretted that he was not an artist in his own right. She would never have freed him, but I was sure that she would wonder if he had freed himself. She would not suspect any woman; she watched him closely, but of those meetings in London she knew nothing.

'When she saw the watch that you were wearing, she must have suffered greatly. At first, when you told me what she did, I thought that she had lost her head—but I was wrong. If she had lost her head, she would have exclaimed at once, she would have asked where you got it—but she kept her head, at any rate at first. But you can imagine how she must have felt. He had been wearing the watch when he disappeared; if you were wearing it, how had you got it? Where had he gone, where was he now? She was afraid to ask you anything, and so you went out of the room and left her to struggle with her thoughts: did you have any connection with him? did you know anything of him? had anyone placed you there deliberately as her secretary? You had just finished typing for her the account of his disappearance—if he was still alive, if you knew anything of him, what revelations would be made when her memoirs were published? If he was alive, would he return? If somebody knew that he had not died, would they reveal what they knew—or demand payment for not telling what they know? You may imagine her feelings. I can. I pitied her from the bottom of my heart. I pitied her when you said that she had come out of that room and behaved as she did. You can imagine how her thoughts would go round and round, making her crazy with fear and confusion. I pitied her when I knew that she wanted you to go back. I knew that she was going to try to find out something of the truth. She hoped to learn something. I did not think she would succeed, for without the watch, there would be no clue for her to follow.

'And then you came here today and ...'

'All I knew was that Anton Veitch was wearing that watch. I had to know why.'

'You guessed nothing?'

'No. But I was beginning to ... to grope. I knew, or I felt, that there was something, fantastic as it seemed, that connected me with

193

Madame Landini. She'd given me a room in her house to keep my things in, and every day, someone went through my coat pockets and my handbag, and read my letters. I knew it was Madame Landini, and I began to wonder ... I was going crazy with confusion, too. When I saw the photograph with the watch, I knew I had to come down here and see if you could make any...' She stopped. 'Didn't you ever want to tell me the truth?'

'Never. Never at any time. But for this photograph, you would never have known. I did not want to take the risk that you would blame your father for what he did. Our past was our past; I did not want you to judge him harshly. Now you know everything, but I am sorry for Madame Landini, because she has always, all these years, held that one small doubt in her heart—and now she is suffering because she cannot prove what she suspects. She is frightened, because she thinks that the past is going to give up its ghosts. If your father were alive, he would be sorry for her, too.'

'If I'd shown signs of musical talent, what would he have done?'

'Taught you. Trained you. Started you on your career. But you showed no musical talent. What more do you want to know? Ask me, and I will tell you.'

'Everything?'

'Everything, without reserve.'

Rodney left the house and walked down to the sea. The wind had been steadily rising and was now almost at gale force. Spray wet his cheeks and numbed them. He strode along the empty, surf-splashed promenade, thankful for the roar of the waves, grateful to be shut by the sound into a world of his own, where he could let his mind recall the story that he had just heard.

Far ahead, a solitary figure battled against the wind. He recognised it and quickened his pace; when he caught up with his uncle, he matched his step to the old man's. Apart from a sidelong glance of recognition, Sir Julian made no sign; even if conversation had been possible, Rodney knew that he would not have welcomed it.

They walked as far as the last glass shelter; then Sir Julian wheeled and made his way round it, seating himself on the bench protected by the glass partition. He wore no overcoat. His hair was wild, his face pinched, his nose very red, his eyes watery. He shook open his handkerchief and wiped them, looked at Rodney and then narrowed his eyes to study him.

'Something up?' he inquired.

'No.'

'You're looking queer. Been drinking?'

'No.'

'Drugs?'

'No.'

'Bad news?'

'Not really. A problem in connection with a book we're publishing.'

'Can't understand why you took up a profession that keeps you at a desk. Not that there's much for young men these days. Wide field when I was starting out in life: India, Burma, Malaya and so on. No future in starting off in any of these newly developing countries; you never know when you're going to be kidnapped or booted out or wiped out or some other damn thing. When I can't sleep at night, I find m'self laughing out loud, remembering the days when all we had to do when the Chinese got uppity was to send in a gunboat and tell 'em to say they were sorry. Funny world, today. Open any magazine, you find it's full of naked women. Read a newspaper, and as likely as not it's the views of some whipper-snapper well to the Left, teaching his elders how to run the country. Turn on the television, if you're fool enough to have a set, and you're confronted by a lot of wild bushmen peering through matted locks and twanging two chords on a guitar. If everybody over thirty was wiped out of existence, nobody under thirty would give a damn. When I was young, it was duchesses who set the fashion; now it's sixteen-year-olds posing with their mouths open—what's their trouble, adenoids? I like to know what's going on, but thank God I don't have to participate any more. Write me off as an escapist. What did you say was the matter with you?'

'Nothing.'

'Your mother well?'

'Yes. My father, too.'

'Don't care how *he* feels. Damned silly feller. He might be able to dock a battleship without scraping its paint, but once ashore, he's not good for much.'

The old man was talking, Rodney thought, to draw him out of his preoccupation, and he felt grateful.

'Don't harbour grudges,' he said. 'My father only had it in for you because you used the money he was going to use to educate us. I had to work twice as hard in order to win scholarships.'

'Did you good. Where's that girl you brought to my house?'

'With her mother, in a house above a shop in Yarrow Lane. A cake shop.'

'That *patisserie*?'

'Yes. She was born in that house.'

'If you know where she was born, you must be interested in her. Are you?'

'Yes.'

'Is she one of these career women?'

'No. Her talents are domestic.'

'Then marry her. I wish to God I'd married my cook, when I had one. That's all a man

197

needs, at the end: a good cook. If you're in any trouble, and you look as though you are, I can't give you money, but I can give you advice.'

'I'm not in trouble. A book that was going to bring in a lot of money is about to fold up, that's all.'

'Good book?'

'Memoirs.'

'Whose?'

'Madame Landini's.'

'Ah. Never heard her sing, not in person, but I've heard her records—who hasn't? She's folded up?'

'Yes.'

'Is that all that's on your mind?'

'Yes.'

'You're lucky. At your age, I was fighting my way out of a breach of promise case.'

'Breach of promise? You?'

'It never got to court. I paid her off. Cost me a lot, but it was cheap at the price. She was a cloakroom attendant at one of the London theatres, forget which. Grasping girl. How far have you got with this girl at the *patisserie*?'

'I haven't started.'

'Then do; she'll make you comfortable. Marry her, and it'll hit your father where it hurts most. Under all that simple-sailor front, he's a snob of the first water. Sea water. Now I've got to get back. Coming, or staying to brood?'

'I'm coming.'

'Then don't talk. I can't walk and talk too.'

They no longer had the wind in their faces. They were blown along, buffeted, sometimes finding it difficult to keep their feet as they were thrust forward by gusts that felt like rough hands on their backs. When they neared the town, his uncle turned away with no more than a gesture of farewell. Rodney went on, finding company in the wild, wind-tossed waters beside him.

He left the sea front and wandered through the streets. Some time later, he remembered that he had not eaten; the discovery was followed by the realisation that he had no desire to eat. Not until the light had begun to fade did he go back, use the key he had been given and make his way up to the room he had left hours before.

There was no sign of Mrs Baird. Nicola was laying the table.

'Your face ... your hair's wet,' she said.

He was taking off his coat. He hung it in the kitchen and with the towel she gave him, wiped his face and hair dry.

'Did you eat?' she asked him.

'No.'

'Well, we're going to eat now. My mother's resting. I made her go and lie down.'

As she spoke, Mrs Baird appeared in the doorway of her room. Like Nicola, she was pale, but calm. Rodney thought the day had aged her.

'I am not going to eat yet,' she told them. 'I'll have something when you have gone. Just get something for yourselves, Nicola. I will make coffee.'

It was a silent meal, but there was no tension; each sat lost in thought. When Nicola rose to clear the table, her mother stopped her.

'Wait, please. Sit down. I have something to say to you. To both of you.'

Nicola sat, but it was to Rodney that Mrs Baird's next words were addressed.

'You know that Nicola was going to leave Madame Landini yesterday, but couldn't give her notice because Madame Landini had gone out for the day?'

'Yes.'

'I can only say that I regard this as a special Providence. Because of course Nicola must go on working for her.'

'Go on working for ... go on working...' Nicola sounded stunned. 'Go on working for her, knowing—'

'Wait till I have finished, please. Didn't you tell me that it was important for the publishers, for Rodney, that these memoirs should be finished?'

'Yes, but—'

'Please don't worry about the firm, Mrs Baird,' he broke in. 'It won't crumble. We'll be all right. As I told Nicola, I never really believed this would go through. It's very kind of you to worry about that angle, but all you

200

have to do is think of Nicola.'

'It is of Nicola that I am thinking. Do you remember how seriously she spoke, in this room, when she said that it was important that Madame Landini should go to the end of the book? It is no less important now. But she will never write another line, another word, until she can be freed from this fear that she is living with now. We, we three, are the only people who can free her. We have got to prove to her, prove without any doubt, prove now and for always, that this watch never belonged to Anton Veitch.' She held up a hand as Rodney and Nicola began to speak. 'Wait, please, both of you. You must listen to me. I have not been resting. I have been planning. I will say again that we must prove, so that there is no doubt any more, that the watch Nicola was wearing never belonged to Anton Veitch. I don't know exactly how we shall do this, but I have one idea, and this is it: The watch has no inscription. I've told you how it was given, when Satz took it off his wrist and put it on to my husband's. Nobody thought of an inscription. It was a tribute, made impulsively. It wasn't until we heard that Satz had died that we wished at least that his initials had been on the watch.' She rose, went to a drawer, took out the watch and laid it in front of Rodney. 'There it is. Look for yourself.'

He examined it, and then glanced up at her.
'What was your idea?' he asked.

'It is a very simple plan, but I think that it would work. I want you to take the watch to a good place in London, and ask them to make an inscription.'

'No,' said Nicola.

'Yes,' said Mrs Baird. 'The watch was made in 1900 or 1902, I'm not sure which. We will say that it was made in 1886, to be given to a couple who were going to be married. We will put on it the initials of my grandfather and my grandmother: *C and A-M*. And we will put the place and the date: *Zurich 1886*. When the engraving is done, Nicola will wear the watch and when she finds an opportunity, she will tell Madame Landini that she is quite certain that only one watch of that kind was ever made— and she will show her the initials. And there is another thing to think of: photographs. Madame Landini has to see those photographs of Hans, who is supposed to be Nicola's father. This is the difficult part—how can she see them unless Nicola is staying in her house? Nicola must think of a way to stay there.'

'Never in this world,' Nicola declared. 'Never, never.'

'In some way,' Mrs Baird went on, unheeding, 'Rodney must arrange this. Nicola must be in residence, as Madame wanted her to be. It need not be for long. Certainly not for more than a week. During that week, everything in Madame Landini's mind would be put at rest. But I don't know how it can be arranged.'

'Look, Mother—'

'No, Nicola. Think more clearly, please. Am I planning this only because the memoirs should be finished? Just consider: can this situation be left like this? You know that it cannot. For Rodney's sake, for your sake and for my sake it cannot. Shall I be able to forget and go on as before, knowing that Madame Landini is unsatisfied, suspicious, searching, may at any moment begin to make wider inquiries? Can you really go on with your life, wearing your father's watch, wondering how many people had seen it on him, wondering if Madame Landini would perhaps decide that you know something of the past? It is impossible. You know as well as I do that something must be done. I know that what I am suggesting sounds silly, even childish, but what else is there? The only difficulty, the only danger is the watch. Convince her that it was never Anton Veitch's, and everything will be as it was before.'

'I have a suggestion,' Rodney began, 'but I don't know whether Nicola would...'

'Say it, then we shall see,' Mrs Baird urged. 'What is it?'

'As I said, only a suggestion. When Nicola goes to work on Monday, she could tell Madame Landini that my parents are coming up from Cornwall to stay with me for a week, so that I'll need her room. Nobody would expect her to rent a room just for one week, so she could ask Madame if she'd agree to her living on the job until my parents leave. It's only an idea, but it might work.'

'No, it wouldn't work,' Nicola said. 'All she—'

'Yes, it may,' Mrs Baird broke in. 'Nicola, you must agree to do this.'

'No. It's what you called it: silly, childish.'

'It's also simple,' Rodney pointed out. 'It's so simple that it might work.'

'Are you afraid to go, Nicola? Don't say at once; think, and then answer truthfully.'

'I'm not afraid she'll attack me, if that's what you mean. All I'm saying is that the idea sounds to me a sort of kindergarten game, and I don't think much of it.'

'But I do,' Mrs Baird said. 'You must agree to go, for one week. During that week, you must make quite sure that Madame Landini finds nothing, learns nothing that she is looking for—which is, evidence that the watch belonged to Anton Veitch. You will take the photographs of Hans, to display in your room. I have snapshots of him; they are faded, but they will do. You must bring them out when you speak to her of your childhood. You must be careful to go over every detail with Rodney, so that she cannot catch you in any mistake. Above all, you have to remember to say that your father had no music in him, never touched an instrument in all his life, but all the same was

204

disappointed when you showed no talent. You know Switzerland. You must speak of it, describe the house which used to be Hans' house, speak of his relations, because they are of course also your relations. I am sure that if you can build a picture for her, and show her the inscription on the watch, she will be convinced.'

'I'll coach her,' Rodney promised.

'I am afraid she is not good at acting.'

'She's an expert at giving wrong answers. I'm sorry it means putting a false inscription on the watch.'

'Why be sorry?' Nicola asked. 'Inscriptions are put on to make people remember, and I'll certainly remember the week I spend in Madame Landini's house. I suppose you're going to tell all this to Oliver Tallent?'

'Tell ... tell Oliver?' He stared at her in stupefaction. 'Tell ... Do you think he's ever going to, anybody's ever going to hear me utter one word of what's been said in this room today? Do you? What do you take me for? What the hell do you think I'm going to do—hurry back to London and call up Oliver and Claudius and Phoebe and—'

'Now, now, now,' Mrs Baird broke in soothingly. 'Nicola didn't mean what she said.'

'Does she think I can't be trusted to treat this—'

'All I thought,' Nicola said, 'was that as he was your friend, as well as being Madame

Landini's agent, your personal and professional sides might get tangled up, that's all.'

'Oh, that's all? I suppose you thought I—'

'Don't shout. I take it back.'

'You accused me of—'

'No, Rodney,' Mrs Baird interposed. 'She only—'

'What kind of girl is it who could bring a man down here, know that he's seen her mother going through hell, and then think he's going out with a megaphone to—'

'My kind,' Nicola said. 'Will you cool down?'

'Please, Rodney.' Mrs Baird spoke appealingly. 'Have you forgotten that Nicola went through something this morning, too?'

'No, I haven't. But I made the mistake of thinking that we were going through it together. I would have thought that there was enough between us by this time to ensure that whatever she went through, I'd be going through too. I would have said that living in the same house, seeing each other every day, trying to work out what was the matter with Madame Landini, coming down here with a photograph that blew up in our faces ... Wouldn't you have said that after all that, a girl would—'

'Yes, Rodney, yes. It was just that Nicola—'

'It's his red hair,' Nicola explained. 'It makes him take off like that. One day, I'm going to hold him down and dye it.' She was on her feet. 'Come on,' she ordered.

'Come on where?' he asked.

'First we clear away these things. Then we go back to London, where you and my mother between you have made plans for me. Mother, will you help me to pack all the clues?'

They drove back through the wet streets, seeing everywhere the havoc wrought by the storm. Trees were down, roof tiles lay in the roadway. There was little traffic, but Rodney drove cautiously. Nicola, beside him, said little. Once, when they passed through a well-lit area, he glanced at her and saw tears on her cheeks. He said nothing, and gave no sign, hoping that she was finding relief from the day's strain.

He drove the car into the garage. She waited beside him as he locked up, and spoke as they were walking to the house.

'Next time your hair goes up and takes you with it,' she remarked, 'you'll be able to call me a bastard.'

'Thank you. I'll make a note.'

'It's a pity nobody but you will ever know, isn't it?'

'You want the fact broadcast? It's not an unusual distinction.'

'Not unique. I suppose not. It's a funny thing; when I was at school, the word bastard always made me think of kings and queens. It seemed to me such a good start in life: a royal father, a beautiful and fascinating mother, and titles showered on all the little bastards, as in good King Charles's golden days. Weren't all his bastards created dukes—and what's of even greater interest, weren't all the female bastards created countesses? It was a subject I liked reading up.'

'Did your mother ever observe you poring over these interesting details?'

'No. I did all my research at school. But it's odd, in the light of today's revelations, to think that I *was* interested. Do I have to tell my husband the dark truth, when I marry?'

'If you're so keen on bastards, why a husband?'

'That's a point. Here's another: if your father ever found out that his ship had been sent steaming up and down the Channel for nothing, and told the naval authorities, could they put in a claim for waste of time and fuel from Anton Veitch's wife and daughter?'

'I'll put it to him as a hypothetical case.'

'When do I have to start being in residence?'

'If you mentioned on Monday that my parents were coming on Wednesday, would you agree to going on Wednesday morning?'

'I'd rather make it the following Monday— that'll be a straight week without a weekend in between.'

'Monday week, then. That'll give you time to perfect the details. One week ought to see the whole thing finished and done with, and

Madame Landini back to work again.'

'If she ever gets to the end of her memoirs, I'm going to take a nice, long break. With my mother. To Switzerland. A sort of pilgrimage to my father's homeland.'

'Your grandfather's.'

'My father's. Have you forgotten Hans?'

CHAPTER NINE

The week that followed was not a happy one— but it was not, after all, Madame Landini who filled Rodney's mind. His main preoccupation was Angela.

It was now known that Oliver's birthday party was to be the occasion on which his engagement to Henrietta Gould would be announced. Though Rodney had allowed Angela to persuade him that she had outgrown her feeling for Oliver, he now saw that he should have looked at her instead of listening to her. For all her declarations that she was over it, he saw that she was deeply unhappy. What for many years he had written off hopefully as a girlish infatuation had taken root. She would, he hoped and believed, resign herself to the situation as soon as Oliver was married, but these days, during which the topic was constantly discussed by the people she met, were proving hard for her to bear.

He was not cheered by Nicola's attitude, which remained one of contempt for what she termed his policy of non-action. On Monday evening, when he would have liked to have heard the result of her application to Madame Landini to spend a week in her house, he had to listen instead to her views on what he should have done to avert the Henrietta disaster.

'Just look at the way Angela looks,' she said. 'Sick. She's trying hard not to show it, but just take a look at her when she comes in—a good, long look. And all through you. If you were determined from the start not to do a thing to help her, you shouldn't have let her come to London, where she'd always be running into him.'

'If I'd thrown them together, you'd now be saying that I should have saved her from marrying a man you think is—'

'It isn't what I think, or what you think. It isn't what you or I want. As soon as I could get myself to believe she wanted him, I told you that as a brother you don't begin to count. I'm certain your mother hoped that when her daughter came to London, you'd do something to get her and Oliver together, instead of which all you thought of was his feelings, and whether he'd be suspicious that you were shoving your sister at him. How can you bear to see her looking the way she's looking now?'

'What makes you think she would have been happy with him?'

'Who'd do anything, ever, if they sat down and thought about how it would turn out in ten years' time? If she'd got him, she would have been happy. And once he'd trained her to pick up a few things and tidy up the place, he'd have been happy, too, and if not, it would have done him good to pick them up himself. Too many people in his life have been treating him just the way you've treated him in this business: sparing his feelings. His feelings have got so spare, you wouldn't know he had any.'

'A man and a woman find each other without help.'

'If they're lucky. Only if they're lucky. Even if you didn't want to push Angela at him, you could have done something to save him from Henrietta. And save him from congealing. Somewhere, buried under all that trendy tailoring, he might once have had a nice warm heart. I'm not blaming you for the whole of this mess.'

'No?'

'No. From what I can make out, it was going on for some time down in Cornwall, and nobody there seems to have put out a finger.'

'If we could discuss something more to the point, could I know what you said to Madame Landini today?'

'I said just what you told me to say. My mother's the producer, you're the director, I just act the way I'm told to. I stuck to the script.'

'Did she say you could go there?'

'She gave me a warm invitation to move in even before your parents come on their imaginary visit. So I thought why not? and so I said I'd go there on Thursday. I know that makes a weekend in the middle, but I'll ask for time off.'

'Thursday? The watch won't be ready until Friday.'

'That's all right. I'll ask her to lend me one of her clocks for a day, until my watch gets back from having its glass mended. I'll tell her you took it to the shop for me, and you can give yourself the pleasure of dropping in on Friday with the watch. That'll make it look all nice and natural. Speaking of watches, will you look at yours just before eight, and remind Angela to switch off the oven?'

'Where will you be?'

'Out.'

He glanced at the clothes into which she had changed on getting home from work: jeans and a shirt.

'Aren't you going to—'

'—array myself? No. I'm going just as I am. It's that kind of party. All-Swiss. Fondue. Only French and German spoken.'

'Anybody picking you up?'

'Yes. A cousin of a cousin of a cousin, name of Sigismund.'

'Sigismund?'

'That's right. Sigismund Klein. The party's

for him—he's over here to learn English. It might get out of hand, so if I'm not around in the morning, you'll know I'm in a police cell with fifty of my ex-father's countrymen. And countrywomen.'

There were heavy footsteps on the stairs. She went to the door and opened it, and Rodney stood up and inspected the large, bespectacled man who entered. The eyes behind the glasses were brown, mild and intelligent.

'Sigi, this is Rodney Laird. We can't stop for a drink.'

'Not?' Sigi's voice was musical, deep and disappointed. Behind him, the door opened. Angela entered and he gave her a low bow and said something in German to Nicola. She translated.

'He says to tell you,' she told Angela, 'that it's a pity I won't let him stay for a drink, as he would have liked to raise his glass to a woman as lovely as you. Now, could I take him away before he really loses his head? Rodney knows about the dinner. Good night.'

Rodney closed the door after them.

'A drink,' he commented, 'would have done him good. Taken some of the German starch out of him. Given him some lightness, which he's short of.'

Angela, turning from the door of her room, gave him a puzzled look.

'He wasn't short of anything,' she said. 'He was very attractive.'

'I'll take your word for it.'

She made no answer, but on coming back to the living room after changing into a sweater and trousers, she reverted to the subject.

'You sounded jealous,' she told him.

'*Jealous? Me?* I'm not the jealous type, for a start. And if I ever decided to become jealous, I wouldn't begin just because a man happened to be well-built and had a good speaking voice. Would you mind pouring me out a drink?'

She did so. She even brought it to him.

'There. It might cheer you up,' she said. 'I'll have one too. I need cheering and I'm not going to pretend—now that we're alone—that I don't.' She lowered herself to the floor, balancing her glass in her hand. 'What I'd like you to explain, if you can, is this: If Oliver had been marrying a nice, kind-hearted girl who really loved him, and who had home-making gifts, would I be feeling any better?'

'No.'

'Thank you. That's what I thought, but I wanted confirmation.'

'What makes you say Henrietta's not in love with him?'

'Oh, Rodney, don't be silly. You know quite well she's been offering bets on being married to him before May.'

'I didn't know. Who told you that?'

'Austin Bates. He knows all her crowd.'

He did not speak for some moments.

'Speaking of confirmation, I'd like some

214

too,' he said at last. 'Would you have liked me to ... that's to say, do you think I ought to have done more to—'

'—throw me at Oliver?' She eyed her drink thoughtfully. 'I don't see what you could have done. Take the situation the other way round: ever since I got to know Nicola, I've been wondering how I could push her in your direction. But it takes all the things I haven't got—subtlety to do it without your knowing, cunning to prevent you from taking fright. So there's nothing I could do, except be surprised that you could live in the same house with her for so long without ... well, falling in love. For one thing, she's a marvellous cook, and you told me once that marriage began in the stomach and ended in the pocket. But if you don't like her, then you don't.'

'Did I say I—'

'And suppose you'd fallen in love with her— then what? Let's face the depressing truth: we're not much catch, either you or me. Leaving aside my looks and your charm, we can't produce much in the way of assets. Like money. None now, and no hope of any, even when we're orphaned. Not that Nicola's background is exactly gilt-edged. I don't know what her father was like, but I like the way her mother brought her up. I'm not complaining, but looking back, it does seem to me that my mother, our mother, gave more of her attention to Chinese geese than she did to me.'

215

'She always considered you—'

'—as father's girl. I know. Which is a pity, because look what happened. List my talents, and what do you find? I can sail like a seaman, I can do any knot you name, I know some interesting facts about gun turrets, I can give you details of every naval engagement the British ever won—and I know the way to run up a quarantine flag. That was all a great help when I grew up and started dating, and even more help when I came to live with you and began going out with city-dwelling males. At first, I couldn't understand it—there was I, one of the prettiest girls in the room, and before I'd got halfway through the battle of Jutland, I was alone.'

'Why blame Dad?'

'Who else? Mother didn't teach me any of it. Maybe I was lucky; left to her, my conversation would have begun with bees and gone on to the effect of cross-breeding in racing camels. She used to come to Speech Days looking as though she'd forgotten to take off her bee hat.'

'True, but when you looked round at all the wigs and false eyelashes, didn't you prefer her as she was?'

'No.'

'Well, I did. You shouldn't complain. As parents, they're well above average, so we're lucky. They've settled into a pattern, but it's not a bad pattern.'

'I suppose not.' She sighed. 'How many people are there going to be at Oliver's birthday party on Friday?'

'I've no idea.'

'Did he tell you that their engagement was going to be announced at the party?'

'No.'

'It's going to be at the Tarrant House Hotel, where Henrietta's mother's staying, isn't it?'

'Yes. Incidentally, Nicola won't be here. She's going to spend a few days with Madame Landini.'

'You mean she's going to live in, live on the job?'

'Yes. Not for long.'

'She swore she never would. What's the idea?'

'We think that if she's on the spot, she might be able to get Madame Landini to go on with the memoirs.'

'Was it your idea, or hers?'

'Mine.'

'I hope it works. I know you're worried.'

She finished her drink, got up to get another and stopped on the way to take his empty glass.

'I still think it's strange,' she said, 'that she hasn't made any impression on you. The other day, I wondered. I saw you standing at the bathroom window, staring out.'

'There's a river view.'

'You can't see it through a blizzard. If it wasn't Nicola you were dreaming about, have you any other girl on your mind?'

'No. And if propinquity's all that's required to rouse my passion for her, shouldn't it work both ways? I haven't noticed her noticing me.'

'She doesn't even turn round when you open the door and come in in the evenings. You'd think—'

She stopped. He had given a wild cry and leapt off the sofa and disappeared into the kitchen. Following him, she stood at the door, watching him as he carried a black and hissing dish from the oven to the sink.

'Did you forget?' she asked.

'No. I remembered, but not in time.'

'Was that our dinner?'

'Yes. Get some eggs out, will you? We're back to one of my omelettes.'

CHAPTER TEN

On Thursday morning, Rodney carried Nicola's suitcase out to his car and drove her to Park Lane.

'Don't worry about anything,' he instructed her on the way, 'and keep your answers simple. She knows I've got parents who live in Cornwall, but she has no way of finding out, unless you tell her, that they don't come to London unless they're dragged, and if they're dragged, they stay at hotels and not with

218

Angela and me.'

'Why?'

'Because my father's idea of hell is staying with people—anybody. And he thinks London's full of—well, let's lump them together and call them undesirables. He can't understand how anybody can live at all, if they can't throw open a window or a porthole and look out over an expanse of ocean.'

'If Madame's windows opened on to an expanse of ocean, I'd throw myself in. I mean out.'

He gave her a worried glance.

'All you have to do is keep your head,' he reminded her.

'It's all very well for you to talk. You're going to leave me at the door and then go and hide behind Phoebe. I feel like one of those movie decoys. Suppose she decides that I know something about Anton Veitch? They can do anything these days, including putting you to sleep to make you talk.'

'There's only one real danger.'

'And I know what it is. You think I'm going to try and fill in blanks about the intimate life of Anton Veitch. Don't worry; my mother can tell me as much as I can learn from Madame Landini.'

'Then with that risk removed, all should go well.'

'I ought to be drawing danger money—but as it's a secret operation, how can you get any money out of D.S. Claud?'

'There's no secret about your staying in Madame's house.'

'Then you can raise the matter of a bonus as soon as you get to your office. Who's going to tell my mother if I get carved up?'

'You'll only get carved up if you get careless and let her suspect something. You know exactly what to do when I bring you the watch tomorrow?'

'Didn't we rehearse it? You said I was action-perfect.'

'Madame Landini wasn't present. If you want to say anything to me, don't phone from the house.'

'I won't have to phone at all. I'll be seeing Angela tomorrow, and if there's any news, I'll get it to you through her.'

'Angela didn't tell me—'

'—that we'd made a date? I asked her to come out with me. You were going to leave her at home by herself, howling. If you make as good a husband as you do a brother, your wife ought to walk out.'

'Thank you. Anything else?'

'No, except goodbye, in case you never see me again.'

He left her and drove away, not without qualms; the scheme seemed less sound than it had appeared in Brighton. Amateurish and awkward, he thought dejectedly—but if they didn't try this plan, what other could they think of that would meet the case? Certainly this one had the advantage of being brief. Today, Madame Landini would lend Nicola a watch or clock. Tomorrow, he would go in person with the newly-engraved watch that Anton Veitch had once worn. After that...

When he reached the office, Phoebe was in Claudius's room. He joined them and explained that he had just left Nicola at Madame Landini's house. Claudius expressed a mild hope that they might soon hear news of Madame Landini going back to her book. Phoebe's comment was that Nicola wasn't the sort of girl who would enjoy a stay in a luxurious mansion.

'She isn't the type to enjoy formality,' she went on. 'And I'm far from hopeful about her being able to ginger up the Landini. In fact, Rodney, my brother and I have decided to face squarely the possibility of there being no memoirs after all. A blow, of course, but here we are, as you see, still upstanding and not at all crushed.'

'I have a feeling Madame Landini will finish them,' Rodney said.

She stared at him.

'Why this resurgence of hope?' she inquired. 'Last week, I could have sworn—in fact, I've just said so to my brother—that you'd given them up for lost.'

'Maybe it's the new feel in the air. Spring. Haven't you noticed?'

'No, I haven't. If you're right, I must do something about livening up my hat. And now I come to the other thing Claudius and I have been talking about. Why didn't you tell us that the staff had planned this totally unnecessary presentation?'

'Unnecessary? One hundred and fifty years of D.S. Claud?'

'But less than thirty of my brother and myself. I do hope you haven't let those poor typists contribute too much.'

He did not tell her that getting the typists to contribute at all had put ten years on to Mr Armstrong, who had inaugurated the scheme. Far from opening their hearts and their purses, they had given it as their opinion that it would be a far more memorable occasion if they were to receive, instead of giving. The smallest contribution of all had come from the most senior typist, Miss McClure, who had pointed out as she parted with it that every mickle made a muckle.

'As you know,' Phoebe said, 'we're to choose between a silver vase and a decanter—that's to say, each of us will take what we want. But if I choose the decanter, it'll look rather odd, so I'm having the vase. I wish all of you hadn't done this.'

'Quite unnecessary, quite, quite,' Claudius mumbled. 'So kind. Didn't dream of any such thing.'

'But we're very grateful,' Phoebe summed

222

up. 'Do you realise, Claudius, that we shall have to say something by way of a speech? They asked us, Rodney, whether we'd like the presentation to be made next week, or the week after, which is just before the Easter holiday. We chose the week after. I suppose we ought to start thinking what we ought to say?'

Rodney left them to think, and went to his room. He hoped that Oliver would ring up and suggest a meeting tonight—a kind of two-man stag party. They could have had a drink together, and Oliver could have come into the open and told him that the engagement was to be announced next day. But there was no call from him. In the evening, Rodney thought of telephoning him, and decided against it; if Oliver wanted him, he knew his number.

On the way to the office next day, he stopped to collect Nicola's watch. He lunched early, on salad; there would be more than enough to eat at the party tonight, he thought, and nothing to pay. Then he drove to Park Lane.

The room into which he was shown was the one in which he had last seen Madame Landini, but this time she was not alone. At a table near the sofa sat Signor Piozzi, and opposite, apparently helping to deal with an accumulation of papers, was Nicola. Madame had a book in her hand; she greeted Rodney with a smile, and waved a hand towards the others.

'Come in, come in. You see, I am idling,

while others work. Nicola is helping Guido, and being very useful, isn't she, Guido?'

Signor Piozzi, rising to bow to Rodney, bowed again to indicate that Miss Baird was indeed being of great assistance.

'Perhaps you will join us at coffee?' Madame Landini asked.

Rodney, who had refused a chair, shook his head. 'It's very kind of you, but I can't stay, I'm afraid. I'm on my way back to the office to keep an appointment. All I came for was to bring Nicola her watch, but they told me she was up here with you, and—'

'—and brought you up here; of course,' said Madame Landini. 'I am sorry that you are in a hurry.'

He had taken a small packet from his pocket. He went to the table and put it in front of Nicola.

'There you are. I paid for it, and made a note to remind myself to remind you to pay me back.'

She unwrapped the paper and took the watch from its box. She thanked him casually and was about to put it on her wrist when Signor Piozzi leaned over to look at it more closely.

'Excuse me, please,' he apologised. 'I have never seen a watch of this kind.'

Nicola handed it to him across the table.

'You've never seen another,' she told him, 'because this one's unique. It's the only one there is.'

Rodney had taken leave of Madame Landini and was at the door. At Nicola's words, he turned. If this came off successfully, he told himself, he would drop publishing and take up acting as a profession.

'Sorry,' he said, and shook his head regretfully. 'No.'

'No what?' Nicola demanded.

'I'm afraid it isn't what you've just said: unique.'

'It is. My mother told me it was.'

'I know. And you told me. But if you remember, you asked me to ask the watch-mender what it was worth. So I asked him. I was going to break the news some other time.'

'There was only one watch like this made,' she insisted. 'I told you—it's unique.'

'The word,' Rodney told her, 'is not unique, but unusual. There are, this man said—and he can be presumed to know what he's talking about—not many of them, but he himself, over the past fifteen or twenty years, has seen four. Don't look so disappointed; didn't you say you'd never sell it because you want to hand it down to your children?'

His eyes were on Nicola, but he knew that Madame Landini had put out a hand and that Signor Piozzi, rising, had put the watch into it. He knew that she was examining it. He knew that she was reading the inscription. Having ascertained so much, he did not linger. When

225

going over the scene with Nicola, he had stressed above all the need to underplay—and the need for being as brief as possible. As he went down the stairs, he reflected that if anyone asked him at this moment, he would affirm that the scheme had been successful. Madame Landini's manner as she looked at the watch had been one of only slight interest—but she had not remembered to ring for someone to show him out.

He drove away with a feeling of unreality. No more than four minutes, no more than a sentence or two. Could so much bewilderment and anguish, so much weight of past events, be resolved in four minutes?

He would soon know. She must, he thought, make her decision today. There would be news when he got home tonight, either from Nicola herself or, if she gave her a message, from Angela. He was almost certain to see either or both of them before he left for the party.

But half an hour before he was due to leave the office, the telephone rang. When he picked up the receiver, he heard Oliver's voice.

'Rodney?'

'Yes?'

'You're all right for tonight?'

'I am. I understand, but not so far from you, that it's going to be a special kind of party.'

'Well, yes.' No prospective bridegroom, Rodney thought, could ever have sounded so dejected. 'I've left the arrangements to

226

Henrietta and her mother, more or less. I'm sorry I ... there hasn't been much time to fix a meeting.'

'That's all right. What time tonight?'

'That's what I wanted to talk to you about. I suppose you couldn't pick up Henrietta's uncle from Paddington?'

Henrietta's uncle ... They were closing in, Rodney noted.

'What time does he get in?'

'Seven-ten. He's coming up from Gloucester and he's staying on, so he'll have luggage, which is why he asked to be met.'

'Where do I take him?'

'The hotel. The Tarrant House. Henrietta's mother has got a room for him there. When you bring him, we'll all join up. The party's being held in the ballroom. You might find it a rush—can you do it?'

Rodney calculated. He would have to leave the office at once, go home, have a bath, dress and drive to the station.

'Barring traffic jams, yes,' he said.

'Thanks. And there's one more thing, if you wouldn't mind.'

'Name it.'

'Flowers. For God's sake don't forget them, or there'll be hell to pay; Henrietta's got this mania for ... Well, I ordered orchids for her and for her mother, but I left it too late for delivery, so they've got to be picked up at Claribel's—you know that flower shop in—'

'Yes. A box containing orchids, already ordered. Right?'

'Two boxes. They won't exactly weigh you down, but I'm sorry you have to go and get them. It's important, remember. In fact, it's vital. Will you make a note and hang it round your neck?'

'Yes.'

'Thanks.'

He drove home. Nobody was in the house. He was out again in record time, and drove first to the famous flower shop, Claribel's, where he was handed two small, scarlet boxes tied with narrow gold ribbon and bearing the name of the shop in gold lettering. He placed them carefully in the back of his car and then drove to the station. He did not get out; he assumed that Henrietta's uncle would be on the look-out for whoever was meeting him. When a large, red-faced, elderly man carrying a suitcase made his appearance, he got out of the car and addressed him.

'General Gould?'

'Yes, that's right. How d'you do, very decent of you to meet me, don't know your name, but—'

'Laird, Rodney Laird. I'm an old friend of Oliver Tallent.'

'Ah. Hope you didn't have much trouble getting through the rush-hour traffic; pretty thick at this time of day, too many cars nowadays, not much fun being on the roads, not much fun travelling at all, come to that. Oh thanks, yes, the suitcase, I'll just shove it in the back. Oh, flowers? I'll hold them; hand them over. Nice touch when a young man takes his hostess flowers, always done in my day but not nowadays, far from it, scarcely a thank you as they go out after being wined and dined, glad to see your parents brought you up so well.'

'As a matter of fact, the flowers aren't from me. I just collected them.'

'Ah. Well, ah. Be glad to get into a bath and out of these clothes, I mean to say out of these clothes and into a bath. Don't know anything about this hotel, my sister-in-law's idea, hope to God she's remembered I can't sleep in a room overlooking the street, too much noise. Understand this is an engagement party, can't get anything definite out of women, especially over a telephone, they waffle most of the time, but I did gather it's this fellow's birthday, never met him, which is odd, since I'm as you might say in the place of a father to Henrietta and a word or two about his prospects wouldn't have come amiss, though they don't seem to think it matters these days, might be time to have a chat with him quietly before the fuss starts.'

But there was no time for a chat. They arrived at the hotel and the General and his suitcase were placed in the lift and taken up to his room. Rodney went to the bar and ordered a drink and was about to drink it when he heard himself being paged. When he identified himself, the small, uniformed boy asked him if he would please join Miss Gould at once in the ballroom.

He did not hurry. Oliver might be under orders, but she needn't think she could push his friends around. When at last he went to the ballroom, he found that it had been turned into a banqueting hall; there were two long tables and, at one end, a much smaller one—at which, he guessed, the principals would be seated. From there, the announcement would be made.

There were already a number of guests. Henrietta, beautiful, he had to acknowledge, in cloth of gold, beckoned imperiously to him and as he drew near, spoke in an irritable voice.

'Where on earth did you get to? I've been sending messages all over the place. The most awful thing's happened. Oliver's car has been stolen. Tonight, of all nights! He's supposed to be here, helping me to receive, but he's had to report it to the police. I'm sick of telling people what's happened. And there's another hitch: he told me he'd ordered flowers for me and for my mother, but nobody at the reception desk knows anything about them. They certainly haven't been sent, even if he really remembered to order them.'

Rodney, about to confess that he had brought them into the hotel, but had put them down and left them in the bar, decided to say nothing; he would give them to Oliver on his arrival, and let him present them.

He edged towards the curtained entrance, said a few words in reply to Mrs Gould's greeting, and went back to the bar. Seated on a stool with two drinks beside him—his own and Oliver's—he kept watch. It was nearly half an hour before he saw him come into the hotel. He went out to meet him.

'Come and have a quick one,' he advised. 'I've got it ready. And I've got the flowers.'

'Thank God. Have you seen Henrietta?'

'Yes. She told me about your car. When was it taken?'

'Between my getting home, and coming out again—less than an hour. There was someone else's car parked outside my front door; usually I make a protest and get it removed, but this time I was in a hurry, so I left mine at the end of the line, close to the entrance arch. When I came out it had gone.'

'Keys in it?'

'Well, yes. I usually take them out, but I was in my own yard, after all, and I wasn't going to be long.'

He looked pale and tired. Rodney, on the point of ordering a second drink for him, glanced at his watch and changed his mind.

'Time to get in there,' he said. 'They're waiting to congratulate you—beginning with birthday greetings. Incidentally, many happy returns.'

'Thanks.' Oliver emptied his glass and stared

231

at the cube of ice left in it. 'Remember last year?'

'Yes. Why bring that up now? We were both heedless striplings, sipping the sweets of life and tripping o'er the meadows with a couple of nymphs. That was Cynthia, wasn't it?'

'No. Pauline. Cynthia was later. Remember the beach party at home on my twenty-first birthday?'

'That's a long way back. It rained.'

'Not at first. There was a full moon. Then it was blotted out, and we couldn't see where any of the food was, and somebody spilled hot coffee out of a flask all over my legs.'

'That was Angela.'

'So it was. I said some hard things at the time. I hope she didn't hold them against me.'

'She doesn't hold anything against you. Will you come to the feast? And here are the two boxes of orchids. Don't hold them like that— they're supposed to be a presentation. And for God's sake, will you smile?'

Oliver, smiling, gave one of the boxes to Henrietta and the other to her mother.

'Darling Oliver!' Mrs Gould had not gushed on his earlier meeting with her, Rodney remembered; excitement, or perhaps it was triumph, had gone to her head. 'A happy, *happy* birthday to you!'

There was a chorus of happy birthdays from the guests, who came nearer and formed a half-circle round the happy couple. Henrietta, after leaning over to give Oliver a playful kiss, gave her attention, as her mother was doing, to stripping off the gold ribbons tied round the boxes.

'I adore, I positively adore orchids!' Mrs Gould was exclaiming. 'Three guesses as to what's in here. One, two ...'

She gave a gasp. It was followed a second later by a low, curious sound from Henrietta. Both remained frozen, staring at the flowers they had lifted from the boxes. And as the eyes of the guests fell on them, a deadly hush succeeded the loud buzz of conversation and congratulation.

It seemed a long time before Henrietta lifted her eyes, and Rodney saw in them an expression that made him take a cautious step backward. She spoke in a manner he had always thought to be confined to schoolboys playing villains in a school play: through her teeth. She was glaring at Oliver.

'Would you mind explaining?' she asked him.

Oliver's face was a study in horror. His gaze went slowly from the bunch of wilted violets she was holding, to the nosegay of dead geraniums clutched in her mother's hand.

'You heard me?' Henrietta's voice was louder, and at the note in it, her mother turned to murmur a warning.

'Henrietta dear, don't lose ... be calm. Please keep calm. Don't lose your temper.

233

Oliver will explain. I'm sure he—'

'I asked you a question,' Henrietta shouted. 'Do you think I don't know what you're trying to do? How *dare* you!' she screamed. 'You ... you ...'

Fury choked her; she resorted to action. She snatched the box her mother was holding and with considerable force threw it, with her own, straight at Oliver's face. One box caught him on the forehead; both fell to the ground. Mechanically, Rodney stooped to pick them up. He straightened to hear Henrietta's next words.

'Get out,' she ordered Oliver.

'Henrietta'—Mrs Gould's voice was a wail of anguish—'do please calm yourself. Please ...'

'Get out. Did you hear me? Get *out*.'

Oliver took a step forward and spoke in a voice hoarse with bewilderment. 'Look, Henrietta, I assure—'

He stopped. Rodney's hand had closed tightly round his arm.

'You heard what the lady said,' he told Oliver in a clear, carrying voice. 'She said get out.'

He led Oliver away. Feeling him hesitate, he tightened his hold. Behind them were sounds— Mrs Gould's prayers for their return, the General's loud demands to be informed as to what was going on, the renewed, agitated chatter of the guests. Unheeding, Rodney marched his charge through the reception hall, held him close in one of the divisions of the revolving door, stepped on to the street and turned towards the square in which he had left his car. He put Oliver in, took his place at the wheel, found he was still holding the battered flower boxes and threw them into the back seat.

'Rodney, I—'

'Quiet.'

'I swear I don't know the first thing about—'

'Quiet, I said.'

'But I can't run out like this without—'

Rodney, now in the middle of the Knightsbridge traffic, drew the car to the side of the road, stopped and turned to face his passenger.

'Do you want to go back?' he demanded.

'God, no! After that? But—'

'But what? Did you want to marry her?'

'No. I swear to you, never. It was to be—'

'—the usual try-out, but this time you were surprised to find she actually had matrimonial designs, right?'

'Yes. I didn't, I give you my word I didn't once mention—'

'—the word marriage.'

'Not when it had become evident that ... How it all worked up to this show tonight, I can't tell you.'

'I can tell you, but there isn't time.' Rodney started the car and drove back into the main

235

stream.

'Where are you ... where are we going?' Oliver asked.

'To your house. To pack.'

'Pack?'

'You're leaving. You're going on a little trip.'

'Trip?'

'Yes.'

'Where to?'

'Anywhere. Anywhere you can't be followed. I suggest Oxford, that little pub I used to put my father into when he turned up.'

He said no more until they reached Belthane Mews. He drove under the arch and past some parked cars. In front of Oliver's house was Oliver's car. They sat staring at it.

'But it ... it wasn't here when I went out,' Oliver said at last in a dazed voice. 'It was stolen.'

'Get out,' Rodney ordered, and hoped the words would not recall Henrietta. 'Go inside and shove a few things into a suitcase, and make it a rush job. I'll give your car a look-over to see if anything been taken or ripped up.'

There was no damage that he could detect. He went into the house, found Oliver still changing, and with an impatient sound, went to the hall cupboard and pulled down a suitcase from a shelf. Throwing it on the bed, he opened it and began to pack.

'Not those shirts,' Oliver said. 'The—'

'Damn it, you're not going to a ducal country house for the weekend. You're going to a pub, and for God's sake, can't you hurry? Don't you realise that in about ten minutes you'll have mother and uncle on your heels? Where d'you keep your razor? Toothbrush? Pyjamas? Sweaters? That's the lot.'

'But—'

'I said that's the lot. Now lock up the house and get into your car. I'll follow you to Paddington. If I weren't dressed up, I'd put you on the train and wait till it pulled out, taking you with it. As it is, I'll have to trust to your self-preservation instincts. If we drive fast, you might catch the nine-forty, which used to be quite a good train—if it's still running. Come on.'

As they drove under the archway, Rodney, following Oliver's car, saw in his rear mirror a taxi driving in. He caught a glimpse of the passenger; there were countless portly, military-looking gentlemen in London, but if his guess was correct, this one was named Gould and owned a niece named Henrietta.

He passed Oliver near the station, drew aside and stopped. Oliver's car drew up alongside.

'Hope the luck holds,' Rodney called.

He turned off the main street and drove back to his house. He put away the car and got upstairs to find Angela not only in, but ready for bed. She was sitting huddled by the fire, gazing into it. At his entrance, she turned, and he saw that she had been crying.

'What's the matter?' she asked. 'Did you ... did you come away early?'

'No. There was no party.'

She got up slowly, and faced him.

'Why?'

He told her. She stood unmoving, listening, and as she listened, tears poured unchecked down her cheeks. When he ended, telling her that Oliver was safely on his way to Oxford, she sat on the sofa, put her head on its arm and sobbed loudly. After watching her for a few moments, he went over, sat beside her and pulled her round to face him.

'This I don't understand,' he said. 'You cry when you think he's going to get married, and you cry still more when you learn that he isn't. Explain.'

'S-suppose he wanted to m-marry her?'

'He didn't. Are you listening? He didn't. The idea, from first to last, was hers and only hers. I might be feeling sorry for her if I weren't absolutely sure that if she'd wanted to marry him, she could have brought it about by fair means. She looks clever, but nobody can say she knows anything about tactics or strategy. And if you'd seen her face when she thought Oliver had played a fool joke, you wouldn't be sitting here howling because she didn't get him. Will you mop up, for Pete's sake? I want to know if there's any message from Nicola.'

'No.'

'Didn't she say anything about Madame Landini?'

'No.'

'Are you sure she didn't?'

'Yes.'

'Don't tell me you both spent the evening mourning Oliver?'

'No. She called for me and then we went out, and then we came back and had sandwiches here, and then she went away.'

'And no message? You're sure?'

She shook her head; she was crying again. He got up and went to his room and changed into pyjamas. The evening was over, let the night begin and it couldn't be too soon for him. He felt hungry, but not in the mood to stand in the kitchen getting himself something to eat. He made himself a large cup of cocoa, put several large spoonfuls of sugar into it and carried it to his bedroom.

'Why don't you go to bed?' he asked Angela from his doorway. 'Tomorrow, you might be able to remember that Oliver's been delivered. Go and get some sleep.'

Slowly, she went to her room. He put his cup on the bedside table and settled himself against the pillows. No news, they said, was good news, but why hadn't Nicola written a brief note telling him what Madame Landini's comments had been when she handed back the watch? It wasn't much to ask. Perhaps she had spent the evening trying to dry Angela's tears.

He would phone first thing tomorrow, and if she couldn't get a clear message to him over the wire, he would suggest her meeting him for lunch.

He sipped the cocoa, scalded his tongue, swore and sat wondering whether it would be worth while getting up and going to the kitchen to put in some cold milk. He was still debating when he heard sounds on the stairs.

He was out of bed in an instant. That wasn't Mrs Major's tread—and at this hour, she was either in bed, or seated in front of the television screen. Would Nicola be coming back to see him, to bring some news from Park Lane?

Angela's door had opened. She was wearing a nightgown that would have won more awards for warmth than for glamour.

'Did you hear someone?' she asked.

'Yes.'

He opened the door. On the landing stood Oliver. In one hand he held his suitcase; from the other dangled half a dozen packages tied with string. From his coat pockets protruded bottles.

'Well, my God!' Rodney exclaimed. 'I left you at the station mouth, and—'

'No nine-forty. Let me in, will you? I'm getting cramp in this hand.'

He came in, nodded to Angela and began to unload the packages on to the table.

'No nine-forty,' he repeated in his normal slow, calm tones. 'And I felt hungry, but I didn't want to eat alone on my birthday, so I thought you might let me spend the night on your sofa, and in case you hadn't eaten, I brought ham and tongue and salad and some rather good Jewish bread and some Boursault cheese which I know you like, and some olives ... I think those ought to be put into a dish, don't you?' he asked Angela.

She brought, wordlessly, dishes and plates and then began mechanically to lay the table. Rodney placed on it the two bottles.

'Champagne. A nice thought,' he said.

'Birthday thought,' Oliver told him. 'I felt that—'

He stopped. From the kitchen had come the sound of breaking crockery.

'Women at work,' Rodney said. 'Go and investigate.'

Oliver went, and did not return. It was Rodney's turn to investigate. He went to the door of the kitchen, looked in, stood transfixed and then withdrew. The picture, he thought, would remain with him till he died: Oliver Tallent at the sink, washing a lettuce—the first domestic task he had ever been known to engage in. Rodney carried the suitcase to Nicola's room and put clean sheets on the bed. He probably wouldn't stay to wash many lettuces, he mused, but here was proof of something he had always suspected: that if you did a thing badly enough, someone was certain to turn up and do the job for you.

They took their places round the table. Angela had scarcely spoken. But when she took her glass from Oliver, she addressed him in a tone of regret.

'If only...'

'If only what?' Oliver asked.

'If I'd known you were coming,' she told him, 'I'd have—'

'—burnt a cake,' said Rodney.

CHAPTER ELEVEN

Waking early the next morning, Rodney followed his usual Saturday-morning practice of taking an extra half hour in bed and then breakfasting in his dressing-gown. This morning, he had company: Angela, also in a dressing-gown, and Oliver fully dressed. Old home week, Rodney thought, as they sat down at table, and inwardly saluted his sister for not having made the smallest change in her normal early-morning appearance—which, now he came to look at it, wasn't unattractive.

When the telephone rang some time later, they were still seated round the table. Angela took the call, put her hand over the mouthpiece and signalled to Rodney. He got up and took the receiver from her.

'Potsy,' she said in an undertone.

At the same moment, Signor Piozzi spoke.

242

'Mr Laird? Madame has wished me to ask you to make her a visit—today, Monday, whichever you will. She has to speak with you. This is all right?'

Rodney, on the point of saying that he would go on Monday, hesitated. There would be time before Monday to find out something from Nicola. On the other hand, it might be better...

'I'll be round about midday,' he told Signor Piozzi. 'Will that time suit Madame?'

'One moment, please.' After a pause: 'Madame begs that you will take lunch with her.'

'I'm very grateful, but I'm not free for lunch, I'm afraid. Please make my excuses. I'll be there at twelve. Goodbye.'

'Is she going back to work?' Oliver asked, as Rodney went back to the table.

'No idea. Why couldn't she have asked Nicola to do the telephoning, instead of Piozzi?'

Nobody could answer this. Rodney finished his coffee, had a bath and when he was dressed came into the living room to find that Angela had made her plans for the morning.

'I'm going to the station with Oliver. I'll come back by bus. I won't want lunch; we're going to have an early lunch before Oliver gets his train.'

They left within the hour. Rodney, standing on the landing, called down his final

243

instructions to Oliver.

'Don't come back until you've got in touch with me and I've told you it's all right,' he ordered. 'Keep in touch anyway.'

When he rang the bell at Madame Landini's house, no questions were asked; he was admitted, and led not to the office nor to Madame's sitting room, but to the drawing room. She was alone, seated at a desk near one of the long windows, writing; on his entrance she turned and offered a hand.

'It was good of you to come, Rodney. I shall call you this now; we are friends, isn't that true? We have known each other quite a long time.'

She rose and walked to a more comfortable chair, and motioned him to seat himself close by.

'This is Saturday, so you shouldn't be working,' she said. 'On that account, I am not going to keep you long. I want to say only this: that I am better. I have spoken to my doctor, and he is willing to let me make the experiment of going back to my memoirs. He has warned me that I must be careful; I am to do a little at a time, with intervals for rest. In that case, you can understand that it would be useless for me to keep a secretary. Miss Baird would find it very trying to her patience to have to work in—how shall we say it?—in fits and starts. I spoke with Signor Piozzi, and between us we had a very good idea: I shall not have a secretary; I shall have a dictaphone. At any time of the day, I can speak into it; there will be no feeling of having to make an effort to work because a secretary is waiting. I will send the results to your office, where they can be typed by one of your staff.' She leaned back and spread her still-beautiful hands. 'Now tell me, do you like this idea?'

He answered unhesitatingly. 'Very much indeed.'

'Good. That makes me very happy. It distressed me very much, Rodney, to break off in the middle, as I was forced to do. When I begin something, something which is worth while—and I hope we can agree that my memoirs are worth while—then I like to finish to the very end.'

'I hope you'll be careful not to overwork.'

'Certainly I will be careful. I will not only have intervals of rest, I will make time in which to enjoy myself. I think you know that His Highness is staying with me? His two little grandsons are going very soon to an English school; their parents are not here to arrange this, so His Highness is doing it all. Of course, Guido is helping him, and they both like to have my advice, so you see that I shall have much to amuse me at the times that I am not writing. And now, there is one other little matter. But first, let me offer you something to drink.'

'Thank you, no. I'm afraid I haven't much time, if I'm to be punctual for my

245

appointment.'

'Are you going out of town?'

'No.'

'I won't keep you.' She rose and pulled the bell cord. 'I only want to tell you that this morning, Miss Baird went away. It is not her fault that I'm changing to a dictaphone; she has worked for me very well, and I decided to give her a little present—Guido has arranged it. I also gave her my promise to recommend her to other employers; this will help her to get a good post, which she deserves. She is quite efficient, though I think there is a little lack of what I call deportment. Do you agree?'

He smiled. 'No, I don't think I do.'

She studied him, her glance maternal.

'Ah! Let me give you some advice,' she said. 'Do not, I beg you, involve yourself with the pretty Nicola.' She laid a kindly hand on his arm. 'You are going to be a man of some importance one day, of this I'm sure, and you must look for a wife who is not only pretty, but of good antecedents. A pastrycook is very useful, but not—ah no!—not as a father-in-law. Try to remember this. You must find a woman like Miss Gould, who was introduced to me at a reception the other day. She told me that she is engaged to Mr Tallent.'

'Not any more.'

'But surely . . . They've quarrelled?'

'You could call it that. She didn't like the flowers he sent her, so she threw them at him in front of a room full of guests.'

'Poor Mr Tallent. Tell him that I have had flowers thrown at me, many times—but if flowers are to be thrown, they must be thrown in a proper spirit. He—'

She paused; the door had opened. But it was not, as Rodney expected, a footman to show him out. Coming into the room was the Maharajah, dressed in a conventional suit but not looking as much like everybody else as he had claimed to do. Anywhere, in any clothes, Rodney thought that he would be outstanding.

'It's Mr Laird,' he said at once. 'Anna, you're not allowing him to go away?'

'Yes, he must. He has an appointment. Goodbye, Rodney.'

Conducted to the hall and ushered out, he found his mind busy. Madame had said it wouldn't do, which was kind of her, because she had brought home to him the fact that it would do very well indeed. He and the pastrycook's daughter had worked together, plotted together, lived together; all that was now required was to change the angle: from brother–sister to husband–wife. She hadn't shown any sign of singling him out from his fellows, but then, he hadn't asked her to. He wondered uneasily if he ought to have given his feelings more rein; perhaps a man's dreams of a future with a particular girl, however vague they might be, should be shared with the particular girl.

On the way home, he stopped at a sandwich bar. He ate slowly; either he had a touch of indigestion, he thought, or there was too much excitement crowding into his life. Or perhaps he was going to get an ulcer worrying about Angela; had Oliver had a lesson that would send him back to old and tried friends, or would he lick his wounds down at Oxford and return to pick up a successor to Pauline and Cynthia and Henrietta?

He got to the house just before three. Mrs Major's dustbin was once again placed squarely outside the Grelbys' door. Once again, he carried it back. Remembering the flower boxes still in the back of his car, he took them out and raised the dustbin lid to deposit them on top of the litter. Going up the stairs, he heard voices—Angela's, and Nicola's. Nicola was back—he almost said home.

Home or not, the voices, he realised as he put his key in the door, were raised—one in anger, one in protest. He paused and unashamedly listened.

'But suppose'—Angela spoke through tears—'suppose he never asks me again?'

'You'll be no worse off.'

'All I said was that I'd go down tomorrow and spend the day with him and—'

'You'll ring him up and tell him you're sorry, but you forgot you had a date.'

'It wouldn't hurt to go, just this once.'

'It would be fatal. For Pete's sake,

Angela, use your head if you've got one. Go to that phone and call it off.'

'He's terribly lonely.'

'Good. Can't you learn sense? You've *got* him ... if you keep your head. He was humiliated in front of a lot of Henrietta's friends, and he came here to cheer himself up, and through the champagne bubbles he suddenly saw you as desirable. If you accept this, the first invitation he's thrown at you in all the time you've been living under his nose in London, it'll be what I said: fatal. He'll ask you once or twice more, he'll enjoy your company, and then he'll get involved with someone else, and this time he mightn't get away. Your one chance, your only chance, is to pin him down while you've got him—which is now.'

'But if I don't go down to Oxford for the day, he'll—'

'He'll be surprised. Then he'll be sorry. Then he'll wonder whether you've got over your passion for him, which'll make him wonder whether he's losing his magnetism, which will make him anxious to see you again and try to make an impression. Go to that phone and tell him you can't go, because you made a date with someone else.'

'But I didn't!'

'All the more reason to make it sound convincing. If he suggests coming up to London, stall; say you've got a full week and perhaps if he rings on, say, Thursday, you might be able to tell him when you'll have a free day.'

'But I want—'

'I know what you want. You want to sit mooning beside the phone waiting for him to call, and ready and willing to do whatever he suggests. I'm only—'

'Am I interrupting?' Rodney asked, entering. 'I would have come in before, but the conversation kept me riveted.'

'Then you heard what she's been saying,' Angela said tearfully. 'I daresay she's right, but he's there at Oxford all alone, and—'

'What we all need,' Rodney said, 'is a nice cuppa. Go and make it.'

She dried her eyes and went into the kitchen. They heard her putting on a kettle and getting out tea cups.

'Everything I told you was true,' Nicola said, from the sofa. 'If she doesn't rush at him, he's hers. I suppose you're on his side?'

'Why does a man have to be played, like a salmon?'

'A man doesn't. A real man knows when he wants a girl, and he goes after her and tells her so, but that's not the kind this man is. Henrietta got him by tying him up before he knew what was happening. If Angela wants him, she won't get him by making it easy.'

'Is this the method you'll apply when you go after a man?'

'I don't go. He comes.'

250

'And if he shows any initial signs of uncertainty, what does he have to do to achieve his object?'

'He has to wait. He has to wonder, and worry, and stay awake at night, and walk to the edge of a cliff and stand there wondering whether to take the next, the final, the fatal step. And now, if you'll excuse me, I'll go and pack. I'm late.'

'What for?'

'My train.'

'Where are you going?'

'Down to Brighton.'

'Without stopping to say one word about what happened at Madame Landini's?'

'Nothing happened. She held it in her hand, she gave it back to me, I put it on.'

'She said nothing?'

'She murmured something to the effect that it was an interesting watch. That was all. If I had to reconstruct—and you know how good I am at reconstructing—I'd admit that for a person merely looking at a watch, however interesting, she held it a long time. Otherwise, nothing—until last night, when she sent for me, thanked me, told me that she and Signor Piozzi between them had adopted a suggestion I made a day or two ago—only she didn't acknowledge that the suggestion came from me—to use a dictaphone, and she would be sorry to lose me, but any time I went after a job that looked a little out of my reach, just refer them to her and she'd fix it, and she had told Guido to arrange a little present, and goodbye. The little present was a cheque for one hundred pounds, which is even better than Angela's record of something for nothing. And that's the end of my glimpse of life as lived by the rich and famous. Now could I go and get ready?'

'About your next job—'

He paused. Angela had come in with a tray, and at the same moment there were footsteps on the stairs—unmistakably Mrs Major's. They heard her pause to get her breath as she reached the landing, and then came a knock on the door. Rodney opened it.

'If you've mislaid your dustbin,' he said, 'you'll find it outside the house. This house. Come in. What can we do for you?'

In her hand were the much-crushed boxes which last night had held flowers. She had taken off and folded the gold ribbon.

'Shan't come in, dear, ta all the same. I just wanted to make sure you meant to throw these away.'

'I'm quite sure,' Rodney told her. 'Didn't I put the dustbin lid on properly?'

'No, it wasn't that. I went out when I seen you'd put the bin back, and I noticed this bit o' ribbon 'anging out, and I looked to see, and I said to meself: "Now surely nobody'd throw away good, expensive ribbon, would they?" But if you don't want it, then I'll keep it.'

'It's yours. How about a nice cup of tea, just

made?'

'No, ta, ducks. I'm goin' to look at a football match on the telly.' She leaned forward to peer into the room, and nodded agreeably to the two girls. 'I'll pop up for a chat another time.' She paused and glanced down at the boxes. 'When I took 'em out o' the dustbin, I remembered that's where Angela works.' She looked at Angela. 'That's the place, isn't it? Packing the flowers, you said. Nice job. I'd 'ave liked to work with flowers, but I'm past it now. Ta-ta.'

Rodney closed the door behind her. An idea, a mere seed, had entered his mind and was growing fast. He turned to stare at Angela.

'You work at Claribel's?' he asked her.

'Yes. I've poured out your tea.'

'Thank you. In the packing department?'

'Yes.'

'You wouldn't, I suppose, know anything... No. I'm raving. You couldn't have had anything to do with it.' He stared from her to Nicola. 'Or could you?'

Nicola's face betrayed nothing, but he saw that Angela had grown pale.

'Drink your tea,' Nicola told him.

'In a moment. Do you know,' he asked Angela, 'what was in those two boxes that were sent to Henrietta and her mother?'

She hesitated. Then she drew a deep breath.

'Yes,' she said.

'You ... you put them in?'

253

'Yes.'

'The order said orchids, and you decided—'

'It was my idea,' Nicola said. 'Stop bullying her and start on me.'

His legs felt weak; he walked to the sofa and steadied himself.

'Let me get this straight,' he said slowly. 'Oliver ordered orchids, and—'

'I knew he'd have to order flowers of some kind,' Nicola said. 'I rang Angela and asked if he had, and she said no. The order didn't come through until the late afternoon, and when she told me, I asked if she'd be doing the packing, and she said she would. So I told her what I'd do in her place. She didn't want to do it, but I made her see that it was the last chance of saving him. I hoped he'd hand them over himself—and he did, and got them back right in his face. And that's all it was.'

'All it was? All it was? It was a rotten, dirty, low-down . . . My God! Don't tell me you stole his car.'

'Don't be silly,' Nicola said. 'We just drove it down to the end of Belthane Street and then put it back again, that's all. And I know it was a trick, but look at the tricks Henrietta played, to get him.'

'But if she'd gone to Claribel's to—'

'—make a complaint? Did she think of the florist when she saw those flowers? No. No girl would. All she'd think, all she did think, was that it was something Oliver had thought up.

254

So she took it out on him. If she ever turned her mind to Claribel's, when she'd calmed down, it would be too late—no evidence, the boxes having been deposited in Mrs Major's dustbin. All we did was throw a life belt at a drowning man. If you want to tell him, go ahead and tell him.'

'Tell him? Do you think I'd tell him that my own sister—'

'If I'm ever allowed to make a date with him,' Angela said, 'I'll tell him myself.'

'If we hadn't thought of doing something, who would have saved him?' Nicola asked.

'Not you. You're the originator of the phrase "stew in your own juice". Your policy is to—'

She broke off; the telephone had rung. Rodney went to answer, and at his first words, Angela went across the room and stood beside him.

'Father? Yes, Rodney here.'

As always, when his father spoke, there was no waste of words.

'Your Uncle Julian died this morning. Your mother is travelling up tonight. I can't go with her because I'm down with flu; she was, too, until a day or so ago, so it's a pity she has to go travelling in this weather. Her train will arrive at eight-five tomorrow. Meet her, please, and take her to a comfortable hotel and see that she has a rest and some breakfast before driving down with you to Brighton. I take it you're able to go to the funeral with her?'

'Yes. How did you get the news?'

'The police. He collapsed during a walk along the cliffs. Your mother will give you more details. Remember, eight-five. Goodbye.'

Rodney put down the receiver.

'Uncle Julian's dead, and Mother's coming up for the funeral,' he told Angela.

'Not Father?'

'No. He's down with flu. Mother's coming on a night train. I'll have to leave early in the morning; her train gets in just after eight.'

'Shall I go too? To the funeral, I mean.'

He considered.

'No,' he decided. 'There's no need for you to go.'

'Will you bring Mother back here when it's over?'

'I'll try, but you know as well as I do that she'll insist on going straight home.'

'I'm sorry about your uncle,' Nicola said. 'I'm glad you took me to see him.'

'So am I.' He frowned. 'I wish the weather would warm up. Mother was down with flu a couple of days ago.'

But there was no noticeable difference in the temperature when his alarm woke him next morning. He left Angela sleeping. As he went down the stairs, Mrs Major, in a red woollen dressing-gown, was taking in the milk.

'Where you off to so early?' she asked in surprise.

'A funeral. My uncle's.'

She looked at his overnight case.

'Going far?'

'Brighton. Goodbye.'

He walked out of the house. As he turned in the direction of the garage, the door of the house next door opened. From it came stumbling a wild-eyed figure, pyjama-clad, barefoot. It was Peter Grelby. He ran blindly towards Rodney, almost knocking him over. Rodney caught him by the arm.

'What's wrong?' he asked.

'Priss,' her husband panted. 'Started off. Jumped the gun. Got to phone Doctor Larrander. Urgent. For God's sake—'

From the top step, Mrs Major spoke commandingly.

'Ere, what's all this?'

'Emergency,' Rodney said briefly. 'Baby in a hurry. I'll do the phoning, Peter; you get back to Priss.'

But Peter, unhearing or unheeding, was on his heels as he re-entered the house.

Mrs Major placed her day's supply of milk on the doorstep. She let Rodney pass her without impeding his progress; as the panting Peter reached her, she put out a hand and barred his way.

'That's orl right,' she said calmly. ''E's doin' the phoning. You're comin' with me, back to yore wife. I 'aven't brought dozens of babies into this world without knowin' somethink about it. Now you come along with me, nice

257

an' quiet. Pull yourself together, or you'll frighten 'er. No need to lose yore 'ead. Look at you, nothin' on your feet. She's a fine, 'ealthy girl an' she'll 'ave it out and done with in no time. Smooth back yer 'air; you don't want to look like this, do you, the first time the baby lays 'is eyes on you? Now remember yore wife's dependin' on you to buck 'er up. Come on.'

Rodney came down in time to see them closing the door of Number 9. He walked thoughtfully to the garage; birth and death, one gone, one to come...

He reached the station just as the train was due. He parked his car and stood watching his mother walking down the platform towards him—an older, more angular Angela.

'Rodney, my dear. I'm sorry to have brought you out so dreadfully early. How are you?'

'I'm fine, Mother. Just this one case?'

'Yes, and very light.' She let him take it from her. 'With so few porters these days, it's silly to bring more than one can carry, and you know how your father hates using porters even when they're available. You know he's down with flu?'

'Yes. And you're just up.'

'Mine was a very mild dose. I wondered if Angela would come with you. I'm glad she didn't.'

They walked together to his car.

'Who found him?' Rodney asked.

'A man who was taking his dogs for a walk.

258

There was a very strong wind, so there weren't many people about. This man found your uncle.'

'Alive?'

'No. A heart attack. I'm glad he went quickly. The police were notified and there wasn't much difficulty about identification because he was known by name and by sight to so many people. Your father advised me to telephone his lawyers as soon as their office opens this morning.'

'I'll do the phoning while you're resting. Who are they?'

'Creed, Boyd and Waring. Ask for Mr Waring. It's not old Mr Waring any more; it's his son, but he'll know all about your uncle. The old man used to deal with all your grandfather's affairs. When did you last see your uncle?'

'Last week. I met him out walking.'

'Did you get into the house any more?'

'Yes. I took a girl to see him. He wasn't pleased, but he came round, and in the end he even showed her his railway. You're going to get a surprise when you see it. It's an incredible lay-out.'

'I doubt if it'll be more complex than the sets he used to have before he went out to India. Even then, he had to have a special room to put down his lines. The trains were never toys; even as a very small boy, he insisted on model engines.'

259

'I don't know what's to be done with all the hundreds of feet of track he's got laid down in the house.'

'Perhaps he's left it all to some institution.'

'What institution wants giant-sized toy trains? What institution can rope off six great rooms to house a railway system? And who's going to do all the wiring-up? There's a control board that takes up half a wall.'

'Poor Julian. While other boys were reading adventure stories, he was reading railway timetables.' She looked out at the hotel at which he had stopped. 'This looks nice. Did you book a room?'

'Yes.'

They had breakfast together, and then he sent her up to her room to rest. He telephoned the lawyers at Brighton, and after being passed through a protective screen of secretaries, spoke to Mr Waring, who was businesslike to the point of brusqueness. He made an appointment for four o'clock that afternoon, and rang off. Rodney thought he was not going to like Mr Waring. He made another telephone call to book two rooms in a hotel not far from Victoria Lodge.

His mother came down looking rested, and he suggested setting off at once, and stopping for lunch on the way. They did not speak much on the journey, and it was only as they neared Brighton that she spoke again of her brother.

'Your father never liked him, even before the

quarrel,' she said. 'Julian had gone out to India before I married—as you know, he was a good deal older than I was.'

'Fifteen years?'

'Fourteen. When your grandparents died, he kept on the Brighton house, and for a time he even kept a skeleton staff in it. Even when there were no servants and no more money, he refused to sell or to let the house.'

'I'm not surprised. He wanted room to fix up his rolling stock.'

'The only thing I regret was not being able to buy some of our old furniture. I often wonder who bought it. He also had some very good things he'd brought back from India.'

'Speaking of India, did you ever hear him mention a place called Hardanipur?'

A glance told him that she had turned in her seat and was staring at him in astonishment.

'Never,' she said with emphasis. 'He would never have mentioned it, and certainly your father and I wouldn't have mentioned it when he was around. Surely he didn't speak to you about Hardanipur?'

'Now I come to mention it, he didn't seem to want to linger on the subject.'

'But what brought it up?'

'There was, there still is, a Maharajah staying with Madame Landini. An old and close friend. When I heard he was the Maharajah of Hardanipur, the name rang a bell, and I knew I must have heard it from

261

Uncle Julian. But he said, and now you say, that I didn't.'

'It just shows you what children hear when you think they're not listening. You couldn't have been more than four or five the last time your father and I discussed Hardanipur. Imagine your carrying the name through all these years!'

'Uncle Julian told me he was the Resident there.'

'And what else did he say?'

'Not much. Was there more?'

'A good deal more.'

'But he didn't go into it. Why not?'

'Because it was a very discreditable episode in his career. He was sent to Hardanipur to keep an eye on the Maharajah. It was known that the Maharajah had succeeded in sending several millions, certainly not less than thirty, out of the country, as well as his famous diamonds. The point was that he wasn't confining himself to his private funds; he was digging deep into the revenues of the State. There were other things, too, which needed looking into; the Maharajah's goings-on were no credit to his Harrow and Cambridge education. Julian was there for a year. He was installed in a palace nearly as grand as the Maharajah's, and had a personal bodyguard and several elephants and I dare say some dancing girls, too. He and the Maharajah became great friends. Instead of your uncle exerting a western influence, which was what he'd been sent there for, the Maharajah exerted a very eastern one. At the end of the year, your uncle was recalled and reprimanded. I don't think anybody really found out exactly what had gone on during the year he was in Hardanipur, but it was felt that it would be better not to inquire. The only reason your father and I heard anything about it was because some of the facts leaked through a member of the Maharajah's suite, and filtered through to us. Your father thought that Julian ought to have lost his job, but he didn't, and in time he even got his knighthood. But that was the foundation for your father's dislike, even before he juggled away my inheritance—and his own. What time did you say our appointment at the lawyers' was fixed for?'

'Four o'clock.'

'Would it have been quite, quite impossible for us to have stayed at Victoria Lodge?'

'Yes, Mother, it would.'

'I should have liked to have stayed in it just once more. I was born in the room above where you say your uncle has his control board. So, for that matter, was he. Did he ever mention the mortgage?'

'Yes, once. I wonder if he sold the telescope?'

'Tele ... Oh Rodney, you couldn't have given him the beautiful telescope your father gave you?'

'I did. I felt sorry for him. If it's still there, I'll

263

take it back. Or you will. I suppose you're his next-of-kin, legally speaking?'

'Did Mr Waring say anything about a Will?'

'How could there be a Will. Uncle Julian had nothing to leave.'

But there was a Will. It had been drawn up, Mr Waring told them in dry, bored, precise tones, a year ago. Sir Julian had come in, had stated that he wished to make a Will but was in a hurry and would go elsewhere if the matter were not put in hand at once. The Will had been drawn up, signed and witnessed, and Sir Julian had gone away. They had not seen him again.

'Two lines only.' Mr Waring's voice and manner became frigid. 'I will read it:

"I, Julian Rodney Mull, leave everything of which I die possessed to my nephew, Rodney Julian Laird."

There was a pause.

'He didn't possess anything,' Mrs Laird observed.

'Of the present contents of the house, I know nothing,' Mr Waring said. 'There was, as you know, no money remaining from the considerable sums which you and he inherited from your father. The furniture, as you doubtless know, was sold some time ago. We now come to the house itself. You are no doubt aware that it was once mortgaged by the Bank.

264

Sir Julian wished them to increase the sum, and they refused. He came to us. We would not agree to a mortgage, but after consultation, my partners and I offered to buy the house, and to allow him to live in it, rent free, for the remainder of his life. I dare say you know these facts.'

'Yes. He told me,' Rodney said.

'Quite so. I was merely making them clear.'

'So what it comes down to,' Mrs Laird said, 'is that there's no money, and the house belongs to you.'

'To the firm of Creed, Boyd and Waring,' Mr Waring corrected in a tone so chilling that Rodney had to fight down a desire to get up and hit him with one of his own paperweights. 'I should add that in the agreement we made with Sir Julian, his heir or heirs were to be given first refusal of the house. This means'—he turned to Rodney, his air weary—'this means, Mr Laird, that we now offer it to you. If you wish to buy it, we are ready to come to terms, but I fear you may find the terms somewhat high.'

'What would I have to pay, if I wanted to buy the house?' Rodney asked.

'It is on an extremely valuable site,' Mr Waring pointed out. 'It is large, and the gardens are extensive and take in the street corner. We should have no difficulty in selling it tomorrow for forty thousand pounds.'

'In that case—' Mrs Laird began, and

stopped. Rodney had risen.

'In that case,' he told Mr Waring, 'I should like a little time to consider the matter.'

Mr Waring's eyebrows went up, and a brief, frosty, contemptuous smile touched his lips; as clearly as if he had spoken, he indicated that boys must be allowed to show off.

'By all means, Mr Laird. Shall we say twenty-four hours?'

'No. The funeral takes place tomorrow. I'll give you an answer the day after—by midday,' Rodney told him.

'Thank you.'

They were shown out.

'You don't change, do you?' Mrs Laird remarked as they walked to the car. 'Just because you don't like a person's manner is no reason for leaving the impression that you can produce forty thousand pounds.'

'Or even forty. He knew, but he couldn't say so, so now he can wait forty-eight hours before closing with his customer. That'll teach him not to twitch his nose contemptuously when speaking of his betters, as for instance my uncle and your brother.'

'He was simply being businesslike.'

'He didn't think it worth while disguising from us the fact that he considered Uncle Julian a demented old dodderer.'

'According to most people, your uncle *was* a demented old dodderer. It was nice of them to buy the house and let him live rent free.'

266

'Nice? *Nice?* It was the best stroke of business they ever did, the stinking sharks. I'm willing to bet they bought at fifteen or twenty thousand. They've doubled their money. *Nice?*'

'Very well then, not nice.'

'Right. And was that wart of a Waring donating his time just now? He was not. We were buying it. He must have charged Uncle Julian a fat fee for drawing up those two lines, and we'll have to pay him a fat fee for reading them out to us. One of these days, somebody'll lean across his desk and wipe him out—all but the sneer. That'll stay, like the Cheshire cat's grin. Do you want to go back to the hotel for tea, or would you like to go straight . . . Well, to see Uncle Julian's body?'

'I don't think "like" is the word. I don't want any tea.'

* * *

There were more people than Rodney expected at the funeral; he felt he could hardly call them mourners. There were old members of the once-large staff of servants. There were representatives of civic bodies; there were the three heads of the firm of Creed, Boyd and Waring. A puzzling note was introduced by a small group of sea scouts, smart and solemn under a youthful leader. At the conclusion of the ceremony, Rodney stood beside his mother and exchanged a few words with all those who had been present. Then they were alone. They walked slowly to the car.

'Do you want to go to the house again?' Rodney asked.

'Not at this moment. I'd like to look round it tomorrow, before we leave. Did you notice when we were there, Rodney, that there was no—'

'—telescope. I suppose he sold it, and put the money into more rolling stock.'

'I dare say.'

'I'll take you back to the hotel and then I'll go to the house and do a bit of clearing-up. You can spend some time there tomorrow, while I go and tell Mr Waring that I've decided to invest my forty thousand pounds in something else.'

'Will you ask his advice as to what should be done with the railway?'

'I won't ask his advice about anything. When I've left his office, I'll go round a few schools—after all, this part of the country is stiff with schools. One of them might have an out-house they could make into a railway depot.'

'Will you ask for any payment?'

'Payment? Mother, if somebody doesn't ask me to pay for dismantling all those lines, I'll be surprised.'

'But look what your uncle spent on it!'

'We don't know what he spent on it.'

'Oh Rodney, don't be silly! Those engines are all beautifully-produced, specially-ordered models. They're worth a lot of money.'

'They were—to Uncle Julian.'

He left her at the hotel and drove to Victoria Lodge. Approaching it, he saw with surprise that a car was standing at the gate. The surprise was greater as he drew near and recognised it. It was Madame Landini's Rolls-Royce.

Madame Landini—here? It was impossible, but that was her car, and her chauffeur was standing beside it. Rodney returned the man's greeting and was about to ask him whether Madame was here, when he saw coming down the drive two figures: Signor Piozzi and the Maharajah. He pushed open the gate and went to meet them, but before he could speak, the Maharajah had addressed him.

'Mr Laird, if I had known that you were related to Sir Julian, I wouldn't have let you go away from Madame's without talking to me. Did you know that he and I were great friends?'

'Not until my mother told me yesterday, sir. Did you come down to see him?'

'I had two objectives. I had to see a school a few miles from here—my grandsons are to enter next term. Having finished with the school, I decided to call on your uncle. On the door was a notice—I have just read it—to say that he was dead. The notice gave your name, and the name of your hotel. I was going to drive there in the hope of seeing you and talking to you about him. We hadn't met, he and I, for over thirty years.'

Rodney had turned; the three men were walking slowly back to the gate. The Maharajah continued to speak in a reminiscent tone.

'It was another life, Mr Laird. A forgotten life. But your uncle would not have forgotten his visit to me. It was of course a visit made officially, in the course of his duties, but it didn't remain official for long. Did he ever tell you . . . No, of course not. If he had ever spoken of me, you would have mentioned him to me when we met at Madame Landini's.' He paused and glanced over his shoulder. 'This is a pleasant house. Had he lived in it for long?'

'He was born in it. He always refused to let it or sell it.'

'How did he die?'

'He had a heart attack while he was out walking.'

'A good end; quick and I trust painless. I'm more sorry than I can say that I didn't come down to see him before.' He rested a hand on the gate. 'He was an unusual man—I suppose you knew that?'

'Yes, I did, sir.'

'You were fond of him?'

'Yes.'

'So was I. He was sent, you know, to reform me. I was behaving in a very un-English way. He was to give me good advice, and keep me

270

from misbehaving. He was to remonstrate with me. Instead of that, we became friends. Good friends. We found that we had a great many tastes in common—the usual things like hunting, of course, but also something else which I never met in any other man, before or since. I'm speaking of his extraordinary interest in, his extraordinary knowledge of, railway systems. Did he ever tell you ... No. I don't suppose he told many stories of Hardanipur. I'm afraid he got into trouble when they recalled him. It was a—what's the expression?—a blot on his career. He promised to write to me, but he never answered my letters. I think someone conveniently forgot to forward them to him. Do you know what he did, he and I, in Hardanipur? We built a model railway. I mean a real railway, a railway in which my small sons could travel. It ran from your uncle's palace to mine. Then we extended it. We had a tunnel constructed. The trains came out of the tunnel into a clearing I had made in the jungle, and then the trains ran round a large, very beautiful lake, so beautiful that we decided to call it the Hardanipur Scenic Railway. The Viceroy prolonged his visit to advise on a branch line we thought of building. If you think that sounds an absurd, a crazy thing for two grown men to have done, then that's just what it was, but I'm glad to say that first my sons, and now my grandsons, are victims of the same mania. I wonder, I wonder if your uncle ever thought of those days, and recalled the Hardanipur Scenic Railway?'

'I'm quite certain he did, sir.'

'You mean that he kept his interest in trains, and everything to do with trains?'

'Yes. In fact, he had a kind of railway system in the house.'

'This house?'

'Yes.'

'What happened to it?'

'It's still there, sir. Have you time to look?'

'Time? If I hadn't, I'd make time. Guido, you come and look too.'

He was still at the controls when darkness began to fall. He had sent every one of the trains on its way. His coat was off, and he had removed his shoes to facilitate stepping on to the allotted spaces. He had set Signor Piozzi to drawing up accurate timetables. He had, with Rodney's permission, put an extra station on the Darjeeling–Himalayan Railway. When Signor Piozzi, with great courage, reminded him that he must be back in London for dinner, he had to say it several times before his words penetrated the railwayman's absorption. Then the Maharajah sighed. He allowed Rodney to help him on with his coat. Signor Piozzi helped him to lace his shoes. Together the three men went out into the dusk, and Rodney locked the door behind him.

'For that,' the Maharajah said slowly, when they reached the gate, 'I shall never cease to be grateful to you, Mr Laird. Mr Laird? You are Sir Julian's nephew, which means that you are almost mine. I thank you, Rodney. You've given me more pleasure than I've enjoyed since they decided I was a bad influence, and took your uncle away. Tell me, who has bought it?'

'Bought it, sir?'

'The railway. Didn't you say just now, in the house, that the railway had been sold?'

'No, sir. I said the furniture had been sold.'

'Ah. You mean that you're going to keep the railway.'

'I'm afraid that's impossible, sir. I've nowhere to keep it.'

The Maharajah, who had been about to walk through the gate held open by the chauffeur, halted.

'I don't understand,' he said. 'As far as I know, Sir Julian never married. Surely you are his heir?'

'Yes, sir.'

'Then obviously, this house is yours. Even if you had a very large family, in time, you would not need all those rooms. So there's enough room for the railway.'

'There would be, sir, if I could have kept the house. But it's up for sale.'

'This house?'

'Yes.'

'The house is up for sale?'

'Yes.'

'And as you have nowhere to keep the

railway, are you also going to sell that?'

'Well, I was going to offer it to—'

'Don't offer it. Don't offer it to anybody. Let me get this quite clear. Guido, you will please listen attentively. The house is for sale?'

'Yes, sir. But I'm afraid the price—'

'How much?' demanded His Highness.

'Forty thousand pounds.'

'I shall buy it,' the Maharajah said without a moment's hesitation, 'on condition that you will also sell me the railway. Is that a deal?'

'I ... I'd very much like to think of you here, sir.'

'I can only be here if you sell the house to me. I shall use it when I come to visit my grandsons. We won't discuss the price of the railway; Guido will arrange that with you. Remember, when you fix your price, that money can't be measured against the pleasure I got from my friendship with your uncle. I'm sorry I came too late to see him.'

He shook Rodney's hand, his other laid in a fatherly manner on his shoulder.

'The house and the railway are mine. Guido will see to everything. Can you imagine, Rodney, the excitement of my grandsons when I show them those trains? I shall see you when you get back to London. We'll meet again soon—why isn't there a short way of saying that in English? There isn't—so *au revoir, auf Wiedersehen*—or as Guido would say, *arrivederci.*'

274

Rodney stood watching the car out of sight. 'And likewise salaam,' he murmured in fervent thanksgiving.

CHAPTER TWELVE

'I don't believe it,' Mrs Laird said firmly.

'Neither do I. But it's true.'

'Rodney, you must have got it all wrong. People don't go round waving a hand and saying: "I'll buy that". Not when it costs forty thousand pounds.'

'People like us don't. Maharajahs do. Why don't you believe it? Wasn't it only yesterday that you were telling me about all his millions, not to mention his diamonds?'

'But it's ... it's absurd.'

'I agree. But think how much I'm going to enjoy calling on Mr Waring tomorrow. I shall inform him that I've bought the house. That'll shake him.'

'But won't you explain?'

'No. Guido'll pay the money into my bank account, and as soon as the bank manager has recovered consciousness, I'll take it out again and hand it over to Waring and Co.'

'Guido? Oh, the Italian accountant. You're not going to get into rather an odd set, I hope?'

'I'm not going to see much of the Maharajah, if that's what you mean. I like to

275

keep my feet on the ground.'

'What will he do with the house?'

'I told you: furnish it and use it when he visits his grandsons, or when he wants to play trains.'

'I'm glad it's not going to be made into bits and pieces. It's such a lovely house.'

'It was. He'll have to give it a face-lift.'

'Who was the girl you took there?'

'To see Uncle Julian? Madame Landini's secretary. At least, she was her secretary until Madame decided to switch to a dictaphone. She lives in Brighton. Her father was a pastrycook.'

'In that case, she ought to know something about cooking.'

'She does. Chef standard. She's also tidy, and handy about the house.'

His mother's eyes rested on him with a congratulatory glow.

'Oh, Rodney, how fortunate you are! As I'm here, can't we meet?'

'Yes. She's down here now. I'll take you to see her. She and her mother live above the shop, but they don't own it any more. Her father's dead.'

'I wish you'd told me about her when I arrived—it would have cheered me up. You haven't told me her name.'

'Nicola Baird. But there's nothing definite yet.'

The glow in his mother's eyes faded, leaving only astonishment.

'I don't follow you. You can't mean that she ... she won't have you?'

'I haven't asked her to have me—yet.'

'But why not?'

'I was going to.'

'Going to! A wonderful cook and a wonderful housekeeper. Going to! Is she pretty?'

'More than pretty.'

'Then surely there's a great risk that somebody else ... I mean, is a girl like that likely to be waiting until you make up your mind?'

'I sized up the competition. It didn't look serious.'

'But I still don't understand what there was against your telling her you were in love with her.'

'There was money, for one thing. She's got none and I've got less.'

'You've got a job, you have good health and good prospects. If she loves you ... but perhaps she doesn't. Does she?'

'I don't know. I think if she didn't, she would have made it clear; she's that kind of girl. As to prospects, I don't know.'

'Does Oliver still want you to join him?'

'Yes. I'd rather stay where I am, but it can't be long before Claudius and Phoebe pack up, and to prevent the firm from packing up too, I'd need money. Real money. The only real money I'm ever likely to see is the forty thousand pounds that's going to brush past my whiskers on its way from Guido to Mr Waring.'

'How much will you ask for the railway?'

'I'll leave that to Guido. Do you want to go and see Nicola and her mother?'

'Yes, very much.'

'I wish,' she said, as Rodney drove her to Number 12A, 'that your uncle had mentioned Angela in that Will. There was nothing to leave her, but I have a feeling he left her out because he always thought she was your father's favourite. It would be just like him to have the last word.'

'I'll give her half the proceeds of the Hardanipur Railway. That ought to pay for a trousseau.'

He regretted the word the moment it was out. But it was too late to withdraw it; his mother had seized on it.

'Trousseau? Do you mean Angela—'

'No. Nothing definite. Oliver's engagement fell apart and he spent his birthday evening with Angela and myself and two bottles of champagne. Then he went down to Oxford, and began to show signs of missing her. Probably on the rebound. If it keeps up, the thing will be to prevent her from making things too easy for him. I know you're against what you call shilly-shallying, but he's been dilly-dallying with a number of women, so I hope Angela won't fall into his arms.'

'If I'd behaved like that with your father—
not making things too easy, as you put it—I
would never have married him. That's to say, I
would have lost the chance.'

'If you were back where you started, would
you still have him?'

'Oh, Rodney, yes! There can't be a more
difficult man alive, but I'm not very easy to live
with myself. We've both had a lot to bear.
That's what there's so little of nowadays—
making a marriage come off in spite of
everything. Today, there's no question of
taking the rough with the smooth. To have
stayed together and made it work is quite a
feat.'

'Is that the voice of the turtle?'

'Don't joke. Marriage is a serious matter.'

'Only if you're married to Father. Here we
are.'

They were at the door of Number 12A. But
before Rodney could get out of the car, a
woman emerged from the *patisserie*. If he was
thinking of knocking, she told him, she could
save him the trouble. Mrs Baird and her
daughter had gone that afternoon to
Switzerland. For how long? She was unable to
say.

They drove away in silence. Mrs Laird was
not a woman who could utter the words 'I told
you so'—but they hung in the air and buzzed in
Rodney's ears. They reached the hotel, and for
the rest of that day, and part of the next, there

remained nothing but the instructions to be given to the lawyers, and the closing of the house. As soon as they had had lunch, they left Brighton.

As he had anticipated, his mother refused to stay in London; she wanted to meet Angela somewhere for dinner, after which she would take the night train down to Cornwall.

Angela joined them in a Soho restaurant, and listened to an account of all that had taken place.

'What about the *Religions of the World*?' she asked. 'Those great heavy books Nicola talked about. What did you do with them?'

'Donated them to the local library,' Rodney told her. 'Did Nicola say anything about going to Switzerland?'

'Switzerland? No, not a word. But she took all her things out of the house.'

Rodney put down his knife and fork.

'She what?'

'Took away all her things. She said she wanted to leave her room free, in case Mother decided to stay in London. And I suppose she thought that if Oliver was always going to be around, she'd rather be out of the way.'

'Rodney told me that Oliver was down at Oxford,' Mrs Laird said.

'That's right; he was. He isn't any more. He wanted me to go down, but I wouldn't, so he came back, but he couldn't get into his own house because Henrietta still had a key and

280

didn't seem to want to give it back, but he sent his secretary round, and got it, and then he went home.'

'Did Nicola leave any message for me?'

'No. She only said she'd ring you one day to find out how the memoirs were getting on.'

It was not, he thought, much of a dinner; the food seemed to him tasteless, and he was surprised to see his mother and sister enjoying it.

After putting his mother on the train, he drove back with Angela to River Street. He stopped the car at the door of the house, and she spoke in surprise.

'Aren't you going round to the garage?'

'No.' He was out of the car and going into the house. She called to him.

'Rodney, you've left your suitcase.'

'I'll be down in a minute.'

She followed him upstairs, to find him searching the drawers of his desk.

'Where the hell ... Oh, got it.'

'*Passport?*' Angela exclaimed in astonishment. 'Passport what for?'

'For crossing frontiers. What else?'

'You're going to—'

'—Switzerland. Right.'

'Then let me see: It's too late to ski and it's too early to pick edelweiss. That only leaves yodelling. Whose window—'

He was at the door.

'Tell Oliver to tell Claudius I'll be back as

soon as I can. 'Bye.'

He went downstairs at a pace so swift that he was unable to stop when Mrs Major came out into the hall to speak to him. Her words floated out to him as he drove away.

'... an' no trouble at all, an' a loverly boy!'

* * *

He looked down from the plane at the sea of winking lights that was London. He was asleep and had to be awakened by the steward when the order came to fasten seat-belts for the landing in Geneva. The formalities for hiring a car concluded, he studied the paper on which he had written the address. He had been in a phone booth and the woman answering from the *patisserie* obviously had her mouth full of her own wares, so his writing looked like the temperature chart of a fever patient. Chanvier might or might not turn out to be his final destination. His previous experience of looking for her told him that he would probably have to make a tour of Chanvier le Bas or le Haut or le Petit or le Grand.

But there was only one Chanvier. There was very little of it, and most of what there was hung over an abyss—but here he was, in a strange car in a strange street, if you could call it a street, outside a chalet that looked as if it would play a tune when you lifted the lid. And it was dark, and the inhabitants, if there were inhabitants, were put away for the night behind shutters. It would be awkward if he threw stones at the wrong window. The one with the balcony, or the one above with the window boxes? He could, of course, lean on the horn and see what happened; with the echo, it would sound like the voice of doom.

He hit the window boxes twice before scoring a hit on the shutters. It seemed a long time before one opened. It seemed even longer before she came out, stepping through the snow in fur-lined boots and anorak and scarlet woollen cap. He put her into the car and took his place beside her.

'Where?' he asked.

'Straight ahead.'

'There's no straight ahead. There's only straight up or straight down. Which?'

'Up, and then round and round, and then we get to a wonderful place where you can watch the dawn.'

They reached a high shoulder of the mountain, and he drew into the deserted viewpoint and switched off the engine. Then he turned to face her.

'Why run out without a word?' he asked.

'Did I have to give notice before leaving? How did you discover Chanvier?'

'I phoned the *patisserie*. You said that a man had to wait and wonder and worry and finish up by taking a fatal step over a mountain like this one—but you also said that if a man wants

a girl, he goes after her and tells her so. I'm
telling you so. I couldn't tell you so before,
because my prospects were too poor, but
they've improved. My uncle left me everything
he possessed.'

'*Religions of the World*!'

'More. Far more. The entire rolling stock.
More still: the house, only as I told you, it had
been bought up long ago by the lawyers, one of
whom looked down his nose and hinted that I
mightn't possess the forty thousand pounds
needed to buy it. To confound him, I said,
"Guido, you will arrange this," and Guido did.
Are you with me?'

'No.'

'I'll backtrack. In olden days, there was a
Maharajah who ruled over a State named
Hardanipur. If you remember, he—'

'I remember. Your Uncle Julian was
Resident of Hardanipur.'

'What you don't know is that the year he
spent there nearly dished his career. Nobody'll
ever know exactly what he and the Maharajah
got up to, but one of their more innocent
amusements was building miniature railways.
When the Maharajah saw Uncle Julian's
tracks, he bought the lot, and bought the house
too. He didn't even have to stop and count,
because although when he shook off the
Hardanipur dust, he left behind his palaces and
women and elephants and tigers and
limousines, he thoughtfully shipped out many

millions, added to which was his collection of diamonds. The price of the railway is yet to be fixed. The price of the house went to the lawyers. If you'll marry me, we could use part of the railway money for our honeymoon. After that, we'd have the rooms I rent from Mrs Major, my job at D.S. Claud, which might fold up when Claudius and Phoebe fold up, and—'

'—and your telescope.'

'No. No sign of my telescope. He probably sold it to buy more engines. Half the proceeds of the railway will go to Angela until she marries Oliver, when we'll ask for it back again, because our need will be greater than hers. Life with Mrs Major will be duller in future, because the War of the New Neighbours is over. She delivered Priss Grelby's baby.'

'But it wasn't due.'

'It didn't stop to study a calendar. The latest bulletin from Mrs Major stated that there was no trouble at all, and it was a boy. That means she's crossed the bridge. From running the street as it used to be, she'll run the street as it is now. She'll hire herself out as a charlady, get to know the life history of everyone up and down the street, and live happily ever after. Now will you stop talking and look at the dawn?'

It came slowly, and they agreed that poets seemed to have a good sense of colour; first a faint misty grey, and the mountain peaks

285

showing crimson; then a mixture of pale pinks fading to mother-of-pearl, and lastly the world white with snow.

'Morning glory,' he said quietly. 'Happy?'

'Yes.'

'Hungry?'

'Starving.'

'Will you come back to England with me after breakfast?'

'Naturally. If I don't, who's going to make certain that Oliver doesn't get away?'

He started the car.

'Home to mother and hot coffee?'

'No. To the house of Hans, who used to be my father. His sister makes English breakfasts—eggs, bacon, sausages and tomatoes, and toast and butter and marmalade, and honey and coffee.'

He switched off the engine.

'Forgotten something?' she asked.

'Yes.' He took her in his arms. 'I love you. I should have told you so before. I love you very—' He broke off and released her. 'Well, I'll be damned!' he said slowly. 'I bet that's where it went!'

'That's where what went?'

'Don't you see? The sea scouts.'

'Sea scouts? Why bring up sea scouts now?'

'I didn't. You did. You mentioned the telescope, and that's what he did with it.'

'Sold it to them?'

'No. If he'd sold it to them, they wouldn't

286

have turned up at the funeral. Going to his funeral was a tribute, which means that he gave it to them. Good for him.' He took her once more into his arms. 'What was I saying before the sea scouts broke in?' he asked.

We hope you have enjoyed this Large Print book. Other Chivers Press or Thorndike Press Large Print books are available at your library or directly from the publishers.

For more information about current and forthcoming titles, please call or write, without obligation, to:

Chivers Press Limited
Windsor Bridge Road
Bath BA2 3AX
England
Tel. (01225) 335336

OR

Thorndike Press
P.O. Box 159
Thorndike, Maine 04986
USA
Tel. (800) 223–2336

All our Large Print titles are designed for easy reading, and all our books are made to last.